MAMA LEARNS TO DRIVE

Donald Davis

August House Publishers, Inc.

LITTLE ROCK

Published 2005 by August House Publishers, Inc.
P.O. Box 3223, Little Rock, Arkansas 72203
501–372–5450
http://www.augusthouse.com

Printed in the United States of America

10   9   8   7   6   5   4   3   2   1

LIBRARY OF CONGRESS
CATALOGING-IN-PUBLICATION DATA

Davis, Donald, 1944–
     Mama learns to drive / Donald Davis.
          p.   cm.
     ISBN 0-87483-745-6 (alk. paper)
          1. Davis, Donald, 1944—Home and haunts—North Carolina.
     2. Authors, American—20th century—Biography. 3. Davis, Donald,
     1944—Childhood and youth. 4. North Carolina—Social life and
     customs. 5. Teachers—North Carolina—Biography. 6. Davis,
     Donald, 1944—Family. 7. Davis, Lucille Walker, d. 1998.
     8. North Carolina—Biography. I. Title.
     PS3554.A93347Z466   2005
     813'.54—dc22
     [B]   2005041179

The paper used in this publication meets the minimum requirements
of the American National Standard for Information Sciences—
Permanence of Paper for Printed Library Materials, ANSI Z39.48–1984.

AUGUST HOUSE   PUBLISHERS   LITTLE ROCK

FOREWORD

As a teller of original stories based on personal and family happenings, I have put together many stories in which the main character happens to be one family member or another. My own mother, though she appears around the edges of several stories, has never been the central topic of any particular story. Over the years I began to realize that, by and large, the family members who had found their way into stories were those whose earthly lives had been completed. The stories were, in fact, memory containers that functioned to keep them alive once they were no longer alive on their own. The bulk of these family stories came into being while my mother was still alive, so I did not get around to working with memories of her: she was still here!

In the spring of 1998, my mother, Lucille Walker Davis, died. She was in the eightieth year of her life and was ill for less than one of those eighty years.

Suddenly, after she was gone, more and more memories of her uniqueness and of her character began to come back to me. One story in this collection, "That's What Mamas Do," came into being rather rapidly. I thought I now had "the story" about my mother, but I was mistaken. Additional memories did not slow down.

At first it seemed that, perhaps, that one story would grow and grow. I finally realized that, when you work with stories about someone as close as a parent, you assemble a novel of memories rather than a single story.

So the stories in this collection are some of those bricks that begin to build the large house of memories about my mother.

In most of these stories, Mama is not even the main character. That was the way she was in real life. She did not dominate by holding the center of the floor. Rather, she was like a skillful fisherman, standing above the water on the edge of the stream, both knowing about and holding a measure of control over the free life of all the fish swimming, unaware, below. I was one of the fish in the stream over which she presided.

So, she stands beside the stream of all of these stories, sometimes casting only one or two times, sometimes actively fishing the waters of the story. But always, she is the marker past whom the stories flow. Perhaps she is more like the mirror in which we who are characters in her larger story come to see and understand ourselves.

These are not all of the stories that have or shall come from remembering life with her. They are but a sample. My hope is that, as you watch them unfold, you may have the corners of your own "mama memories" dusted and therein find stories of your own not yet realized or imagined.

—DONALD DAVIS

CONTENTS

Mama Learns to Drive 7

That's What Mamas Do 19

Peas and Carrots 35

Jack Marr Builds a House 47

Fruitcake Cookies 57

A Room of My Own 71

Friends Come Back 89

Losing My Name 111

MAMA LEARNS TO DRIVE

Mama, Lucille Walker-someday-to-be-Davis, was born and raised on a mountain farm far back in the Smoky Mountains of North Carolina. Her parents, Zephie and Grady, worked that part of the farm that was not too hilly or rocky to work, using oxen or mules or horses. In all of her growing-up years, there was never a car on the "farm place."

When my grandfather died at age ninety-five, Mama and I were walking over that same farm where she had grown up. Suddenly a question occurred to me. "Mama," I asked her, "when you were a little girl living way out here, how did your family get to town? I know that you didn't ever have a car out here, and it was about sixteen miles to town, even with the new road."

All of a sudden, Mama got a funny look on her face. "I think"—she seemed to be searching far back into memory—"I think that we went to town for the first time when I was about eight years old."

Then she told me a little story.

"One day, when I was about eight, Daddy decided that we should go to town. That would have been about nineteen twenty-six. We had breakfast early, and then he hitched the horses to the wagon. Mama packed up some food and we all got in the wagon. There were only four of us children then. Well, we went to town! It took a long time because the old road was still here then, and it was not paved until somewhere past Lake Junaluska. We didn't see a car the whole way."

I could not imagine what an impression this trip must have made on her. I asked the question that seemed obvious to me. "What in the world did you do when you got there?"

"Daddy stopped the wagon, and he said, 'We're here! You all stand up and look around.'"

"What did you do?" I asked.

"We all stood up and looked around. Then we all sat back down in the wagon and went home! I guess we just didn't have any business in town. We stopped and had our picnic beside the road when we were almost back home." The look on her face said it all. She had been excited, but Granddaddy never was one for wandering far from home.

"I think we went again when I was about thirteen years old."

That was the end of Mama's story.

———

Mama grew up walking about a mile and a half to school each day—a total of three miles round-trip. As time passed, she began helping more and more with her own little sisters and brothers. There were nine children in all, and she was the oldest.

In 1935 Mama graduated as the valedictorian of her tiny high school class. She had been to town twice and had never ridden in a car. All of the county roads were dirt, and hardly any cars ever came through Rush Fork.

At the end of the summer, Granddaddy loaded her, along with her trunk of clothes and few personal effects, into the wagon and took her into town to the train station. There she was put on the train to ride twenty-seven miles to Asheville, where she entered Asheville Normal Teachers' College. She would work her way through school and become the first of all seven sisters to be schoolteachers.

As I think back about that remarkable day in my mother's life, I realize that if I were to fly to the moon, I would not travel farther than she did in those twenty-seven miles to Asheville.

That night—her first night ever away from home—she slept in a room where she could turn off the light instead of blowing it out! For the first time in her life, she slept on a mattress instead of a feather-filled tick made by her mother and grandmother. And for the first time ever, she slept in a building in which you could actually make a trip to the bathroom without going outdoors!

The all-girl Teachers' College had strict rules. Students could not leave campus unless they were in groups of five and accompanied by a faculty chaperone. (She fondly remembered the first movie she saw. On the Friday after Thanksgiving of her first year, all the students walked, with chaperones, to see *How Red Is My Rose,* with Nelson Eddie and Jeanette McDonald. She never forgot it!)

Many years later, during my older childhood, Mama and I rode through the Biltmore Village section of Asheville. You could look up and see the hill-top Mission Hospital, which now occupied the former campus of her teachers' college. As we passed by All Souls' Episcopal Church, Mama remarked, "That's where I went to church when I was in college."

Looking over at the beautiful Episcopal church, I asked, "You went there? But we are Methodists."

"Yes," she smiled, "I went to the Methodist church the first years. I went every Sunday because the only way you could get off campus was to be signed out to go straight to church and back. But," she continued, "before my senior year, they built a place right up there on Biltmore Avenue that made Krispy Kreme doughnuts—you had to pass it coming to and going back from church—so a whole bunch of us became Episcopalians!"

No one was allowed to ride in a car unless they were riding with either their father or their older brother. She had no older brother, and her father had no car. So, if in her college career Mama ever rode in a car, she would never admit it.

After graduation from the Teachers' College, she returned home and got a job teaching third grade in the same school she had attended as a child, still walking the mile and a half each morning and afternoon. Besides her teaching duties, she now had eight younger brothers and sisters to help care for, most of whom were still living at home.

Mama had taught for two years when the United States entered the Second World War. Civil defense preparations were going on all over the country. One of the components of local preparations included Red Cross first-aid classes. Almost every school hosted a series of first-aid classes, available to all the teachers and interested parents as well.

Mama went to the first class session at her school. After the session, Joe Davis, the first-aid teacher, offered her a ride home. Whether she accepted the ride on the first night or after several tries neither of them would admit later. At some point, though she got in the car, and not only did she ride home, she eventually ran away and married my daddy, a banker who was not in the war because he was forty-three years old—eighteen years older than my mother!

Mama fell in love in a 1936 Plymouth, which may have been the first car in which she had ridden in her life! She was twenty-five years old.

When they got married in 1943, Mama and Daddy moved into an apartment in the town of Sulpher Springs. When it was obvious that I was on my way into the world, Mama took a break from teaching in order to perfect her new life as a wife and mother. In a few months, Daddy bought an old bungalow-style house on an unpaved North Carolina mountain road that everybody called Plott Creek Road. Daddy worked at the one bank in town, and since the second bank had closed during the panic of 1929 and had never opened again, it took him a while to totally trust the permanence of his place of employment. For that reason, Daddy wanted to live on a farm with enough room for us to have a large garden, a milk cow, chickens for eggs and meat, a pig, and a lot of apple trees. That way, we would not starve to death if the bank closed.

They moved into that house in the months before I was born, and it was to be home for the first twelve years of my life.

When I started the second grade and my brother Joe

entered the Methodist church-basement kindergarten, Mama decided that it was time for her to go back to teaching school.

Daddy completely agreed, under one condition. "If you are going to teach school," he said, "it would be a good idea for you to learn to drive. Everybody needs to know how to drive in these days. Someday we may even have two cars! After all, we're living in the nineteen-fifties!"

So Mama began to learn to drive.

Daddy was now in his fifties, Mama in her thirties. He was her only available teacher. Our car was a 1948 blue, six-cylinder Plymouth, with a clutch pedal beside the brake pedal and three-speed gearshift on the steering column. I was seven and Joe was five. The two of us rode in the back seat of the car and watched while Daddy became the proud teacher.

Mama gripped the steering wheel of the Plymouth so hard that her finger dents were still there five years later when we traded the car. Daddy, with a grin on his face, tried with masculine, mechanical logic to explain to her how to work three pedals when you only have two feet. (Mama, a schoolteacher, could not do the math and get a whole number.) I sat in the back and watched the whole show while, in those days before seatbelts, Joe lay on the back-seat floorboard of the Plymouth kicking the back of the front seat and screaming with every breath, *"Dooon't let her drive! Dooon't let her drive! She'll kill us all! She'll kill us all!"* It was the best show in town.

Anytime that I have any doubts that miracles really do happen, I think about Mama's driving lessons. The fact that she finally did it is miraculous affirmation.

After several weeks of driving lessons and practice, Daddy decided that she was ready to go to town and take her driving test. She was not sure she would ever be ready, but she agreed to give it a try. There was, however, one last hurdle.

"Before you go take the big test," Daddy smiled at her, "you have to drive through Hazelwood! If you can do that, you'll pass the test."

Hazelwood was a little industrial town that was incorporated on the edge of Sulpher Springs. It had one short main street that ran from the railroad tracks through one block of businesses, then past houses and up a steep hill to one of the only traffic lights in the county. At the traffic light, you had to turn either left or right.

We rode through Hazelwood, with Mama driving successfully, and on up the hill toward the traffic light. The light was green, and Mama turned left toward home. "Do it again!" Daddy said.

We circled through the middle of Hazelwood again, and

again the light was green! Mama was sure we were going home now. "Do it again!" Daddy said.

On the third trip through Hazelwood, Mama's luck ran out! The traffic light was red.

She stopped at the top of the hill, and there we sat. Mama's grip on the steering wheel was deadly, and both of her legs were locked: her right foot on the brake with all the pressure she could put on it, and her left leg extended straight as her foot pressed the clutch hard against the floorboard. Her eyes were closed because she was praying that the Second Coming would arrive before the light turned green, and that if it didn't, maybe her feet would know what to do, because her brain had no idea.

Daddy had the biggest grin on his face I had ever seen, and I watched it all as Joe paused from his kicking and screaming, waiting to see exactly what was going to happen.

The light turned green, and Mama's prayer was half-answered: one of her feet moved! Her right foot came off of the brake pedal and hit the accelerator, sending it to the floor, while her left leg remained locked holding the clutch flat against the floor!

Slowly, with the racing engine roaring wide open, the Plymouth containing our entire living family started rolling backward down the hill. As we started moving, Joe started screaming, *"She's killing us! She's killing us!"*

Luckily there was no traffic in Hazelwood as we rolled backward down Main Street toward the center of town. As the blue Plymouth rolled, Mama's alignment got off a little bit, and instead of traveling in a straight line, we drifted to the left across the street, hit the curb and bounced over it, and traveled backwards across the new front yard of Clyde Fisher's new house. By the time the car stopped, we had pushed two just-set-out juniper bushes out of the ground and back under the porch.

Inside the house, Clyde and Mary Fisher heard a noise and came out on the porch to see what it was. Clyde was the mayor of Hazelwood, and my daddy, who ran the loan department at the bank, had financed the new house. Clyde looked down at my daddy, and Daddy looked up at him. "Well, Joe, what are you-all doing out here?"

Daddy smiled his widest, "Well, Clyde, we heard that you had moved, so we were just dropping by to see how you were doing at your new house!" My memory is that Daddy ended up driving home after that.

About a week later, without any more lessons in between, Mama went to town and took her driver's test. She passed with no trouble at all and came home proudly holding her new North Carolina driver's license in her hand. She was thrilled, but she was also as mad as she could be.

"You didn't tell me!" she started in on Daddy.

"What did I not tell you?" he asked. "Did they make you parallel park?"

"I can do that!" she answered him quickly. "You didn't tell me."

"What? Did they make you start out on a hill?"

"I can do that too! You didn't tell me!"

"What did I not tell you?" Daddy asked, almost in despair.

Mama was ready this time. "You didn't tell me they were going to ask me how much I weighed! And when I told them that I didn't know, they pulled out some old scales that didn't half work, and they made me stand on them right there in front of everybody!" Oh, was she mad.

———

There are two times when, in adulthood, I think about Mama learning to drive.

One of those times happens whenever I happen to be back at my childhood home and, without thinking about it, realize that I am driving through Hazelwood. Then, also without realizing it, I hear my brother saying, *"She's killing us! She's killing us!"*—and I chuckle.

The other time is more important than that. The other

time that I think about Mama learning to drive comes whenever, as an adult, I have to learn to do something new that I don't think I can learn (and usually don't want to learn either). After almost giving in to the temptation to give up, I suddenly think about my mama. Then I catch on.

If she could learn to drive after spending a quarter-century of her life with no experience with cars so that she could drive me to Boy Scouts and to the church youth group and to band practice and to the library and, eventually, even away to college—if my mama could do that, I can do anything!

So I remember, and then I say, "Thank you, Mama!"

THAT'S WHAT MAMAS DO

It was the summer of 1950, and I was six years old. My mother was taking a break from teaching until my brother and I were older. Every day of this summer she would teach me something she thought I needed to know before entering first grade at the end of the summer.

On this particular day we were still at the breakfast table when Mama said, "Today it is time for you to learn to go to the store by yourself. I'm going to give you some money, and you are going to walk down to the Eagle's Nest Grocery and buy us a loaf of bread.

"Now, you are to walk on the left-hand side of the road so that you can see the traffic coming and get out of its way. You are to look both ways before you cross the road to get to the store. And this is what you say to Mr. Cagle: 'I would like to buy one loaf of Colonial thin-sliced sandwich bread, please.'

"Walk back home on the other side of the road, and look both ways again before you cross back over to our house."

We lived about two miles outside of the town of Sulpher Springs on an unpaved North Carolina mountain road that everybody called Plott Creek Road. The dirt road was very dusty, and Mama was certain that every single speck of dust stirred up by every single car that came down the road blew straight in the windows of our house and proceeded to multiply. Her great defensive weapon in her battle with dust was what came to be known in the family as "Mama's Dust Hedge."

The Great Dust Hedge started at the top edge of the garden about fifty yards up the road from the house. It continued down the roadside the length of the garden, then kept on for the width of the front yard and, with only a tunnel that our car could squeeze through, continued on down the length of the cow pasture until our property ended almost directly across the road from where the Eagle's Nest Grocery was located.

The hedge was a combination of privet and boxwood, entangled along the way with cedar and locust trees as well as a great interweaving of honeysuckle. It really did stop a lot of road dirt and even noise. It also meant we could not see out of where we lived.

To me, at that moment, the dust hedge meant only one

thing. As soon as I was out the end of the driveway and walking along the road to the store, my mama would not be able to see either me or anything I happened to be doing all the way to the store and back again.

I gripped the money Mama had given to me and started down the road to the store.

On the side of the road where I was walking, there was nothing but our land. All the way down to the stop sign where the dirt road joined the pavement, I made my way parallel to our cow pasture on my way to the store. Across from the end of our land sat the little store, an early version of a quick-stop shortcut community market doing business to save people the two-mile trip to the real grocery store in town.

I watched the opposite side of the road while I walked past the big hayfield that unrolled itself up to the front of the George Plott house, home of the Plott Hound, "the only hunting dog breed totally developed in North America," Daddy always said. Halfway to the store, the Mehaffey house stood across the road with its high rock foundation and covered porch along the front.

If I had started school and had known how to count, I would have joyfully counted the steps as, with the pride of freedom, I walked farther and farther from my mother's vision and from her supervision as well.

Not one car ever came up or down the dirt road on all my way to the store. I looked both ways anyway, crossed carefully, and arrived at Eagle's Nest Grocery.

Mr. Cagle, who ran the store, saw me coming. He was always on the lookout so that he could step outside to give customers room to step in. The entire building was no bigger than twelve by sixteen feet, and with a dairy and drink cooler in the back and square ice-cream box beside the front door, there was almost no open floor space at all.

Perhaps the greatest elation of the day came from knowing where the bread was. The bread was brightly wrapped in waxed paper, and I picked out a loaf, handling all the others in the process to be sure I had the right one. When I handed Mr. Cagle the money Mama had given to me, he handed part of it back and then gave me more change as well. Now I pocketed the money and started up the other left-hand side of the road, back toward home.

Halfway home, I was nearing the Mehaffeys' house. Just at that moment a car did pass me from behind. I watched as the car eased over toward the left side of the road. A hand came out the window and stuck the Asheville *Times* newspaper into the Mehaffeys' paper box.

We had an old paper box in the hedgerow in front of our house, but we got no newspaper. The paper box was left over from the family who had lived in the house before Daddy bought it. No, Daddy always bought the paper in town, and when he got home with it, it had been thoroughly read through and through. Even though I could not read, something in me knew that there was something special about being the very first person to ever touch a new, unread newspaper.

What happened next I personally did not do. No, when you are six years old you are not personally responsible for what your hands do. At that age hands are free agents with a life and mind of their own. All you can do is look at them each morning and say, "Wonder where you are going today?" and then follow them there.

As my body walked past the Mehaffeys' newspaper box, one of my hands reached up and took their brand new newspaper out of the box. The other hand helped to unfold the paper. Though I was unable to read the word STOP on a stop sign, I walked up the road "reading" the paper out loud.

All of a sudden, from behind the dust hedge on the other side of the road, I heard the voice of God. But God sounded like he had borrowed my mother's voice! The voice of God said, "You better put that back!"

My body went into reverse, and as it backed up, my hands folded and re-rolled the newspaper and put it right back into the Mehaffeys' paper box.

Then, with the loaf of bread, I walked on back home where Mama was waiting for me on the front porch of the house.

Later that evening we were eating supper at the kitchen table. Daddy, home from the bank, was at his end of the table. Mama was at the other end, and Joe and I were each on our own proper sides.

All of a sudden, Mama said to Daddy, "I sent him to the store today," nodding toward me. "He took the Mehaffeys' paper out of their paper box. I knew he was going to do it!"

I popped up. "How did you know?" I asked. "I didn't even know it was going to happen."

"I knew when you were born!" Mama laughed as she announced it. "Because . . . that's what boys do!"

At that very moment I realized that it was not God after all who had watched me from behind the dust hedge. I spoke out to Mama, "You were spying on me, weren't you? You watched me all the way down there and all the way back— and I didn't even know it! Why did you do that?"

"Because," she said with a smile, "that's what Mamas do!"

That event established the contract under which my mother and I lived the rest of our lives together. It was my responsibility and my duty to "do what boys do." I even taught my brother as well as I could! But it was also Mama's job to "do what Mamas do," and she was pretty good at that as well.

When I was in the sixth grade and my brother Joe was in the fourth grade, our family bought a new house. Daddy and Mama purchased the house in the spring of the year, but we were not going to make the actual move until school got out for the summer.

During that waiting time, my brother Joe and I got a present that was so big we had to agree that it counted for both of our birthdays. The big present was a gigantic swingset.

The idea was that the swingset would be for the bigger and flatter yard at the new house, but it came early, and we were not content to let it stay in the box until we moved. Daddy agreed to put part of it together at that time so that we could learn to play with it.

The swingset had A-frame legs at either end with a long pipe between them at the top. Down from the pipe at the top hung two regular swings, a monkey-bar that you could jump up and grab hold of, a two-seated glider affair that two people could pump and ride back and forth at the same time, and a long, polished slide that attached to one end.

Daddy started putting it together, as he said, "a little bit at a time." He got the legs up, then the top pipe, then all of the hanging swings, but not the slide. "We'll save that until we move the whole thing over to the new house," he declared. "When we get it all over there, I'll put up the sliding board and even set the legs in concrete so it won't turn over. While we're still over here on Plott Creek, you can learn to use it, but you just have to be careful."

I absolutely loved the swingset. I learned to grab the crossbar between the A-frame legs and "skin the cat." I learned to climb to the top and hand-walk from end to end of the long main pipe. I even loved to play with it the way you were supposed to!

More than anything else, though, I loved it when my brother Joe came out and sat in the swing in the middle and said, "Will you push me?"

I loved pushing my brother!

When I really got him going, I noticed that as he swung forward, the back legs of the swing would jump a few inches off of the ground. Then when he came swinging back, the front legs would jump off the ground. It was so interesting. It even seemed that, if you kept pushing as hard as you could, the swing would begin to rock back and forth and would actually creep down the slope of the yard if you could just keep doing it long enough.

One day he and I were out in the yard playing around the swingset. I was actually doing two things at the same time: pushing my brother and looking around to see where our mama was. She was nowhere! So I pushed him harder. Pretty soon I was pushing my brother so hard that his entire functional vocabulary dropped to a single word: "Higher! Higher!"

After two or three more pushes, I said, "Hang on! I think I can make you go all the way around!"

The next time he came swinging back toward me, I gave him the hardest running push I had ever given since the world was created. When he went forward this time, he didn't come back! The back legs of the swing came off of the ground, and they just kept coming! Everything went over in a big crash, and everything, including my brother Joe, hit the ground at the same time.

Joe hit the ground so hard that I was sure I had killed him. The fall had knocked the breath out of him and he lay there on his back, unable to move, gasping and groaning until he could get his lungs to accept air again.

I stood there knowing that he was dying and that I would go to prison—or that if he was alive, he would tell Mama and she would kill me. I didn't know whether to run and get Mama, or to run and simply keep running.

About that time he came back to life. I went over and pumped on him in an untaught artificial-respiration sort of way that got him breathing again. As soon as he could talk, the first thing he said was, "Don't tell Mama!" Somehow, my brother thought it was all his fault!

The adrenalin that the two of us had generated by now enabled us to get the swingset back up without any trouble.

That night at the supper table, we were all sitting and eating together very peacefully. Daddy was at his end of the table, Mama was at hers, and Joe and I were on our proper sides.

All of a sudden, almost in the middle of a bite, Mama said to Daddy, "Guess what? They turned the swingset over today. I knew they were going to do it!"

From his place behind the table, Joe said, "How did you know we were going to do it? We didn't even know!"

"I knew," she replied with a smile, "because that's what boys do!"

"It hurt," my brother whimpered. "I could have been killed. If you knew we were going to do it, why didn't you stop us? I think that's what good Mamas are supposed to do!"

"Well," she went on, "I could have stopped you today. Then I would have had to stop you tomorrow, and the next day, and the next day. I would have had to stop you every day for the next ten years! But I knew that if I just let you go ahead and do it once, you'd never do it again!"

"It really did hurt," Joe whined. "Why did you do that?"

"Because," Mama smiled, "That's what *smart* Mamas do."

When school got out that year, we did move, swingset and

all, to the new house. Joe and I spent the rest of our at-home years there, and Mama and Daddy both lived in "the new house" for the rest of their lives.

The new house was not within easy walking distance of a store of any kind, and being on the opposite side of town from Plott Creek, it was not located so that Daddy could drive us to school on his way to and from work. Soon he bought a second car, a used Plymouth that was exactly like the one we had traded in two new cars earlier. Now we were a two-car family.

By the time Joe and I were both in high school and had our driver's licenses, the two cars meant that he and I could sometimes both be out at night, separately, in two different vehicles. It was at this time that we discovered a great flaw of the new house, a flaw that Joe and I had not realized until now: all of the doors could be locked!

Now, whenever Joe and I were out separately at night and we happened to stay out beyond the time when we had been told to be home, Mama simply locked all of the doors except the door from the garage into the kitchen. This meant that whenever either of us got home late, the only way into the house was to raise the garage door far enough to get under it, pull it back down, then go in the house through the unlocked kitchen door.

This garage door was a big, sectional wooden door that went up and down on metal rollers aided by springs and chains. Daddy had quickly nicknamed it "the earthquake door" because it shook the whole house and was so noisy that it seemed like it could wake up the neighbors on either side of us.

By the time you got this door up just enough to get under it, crept in, closed the door again, and got to the kitchen, Mama was out of bed and in the kitchen with her watch in one hand (even though there was a perfectly good clock on the wall) and her notebook in the other. She was waiting to write down which of us was late and how late we were so that she could subtract that much time from our lives later on.

As a teenager I couldn't live like that! Pretty soon I was checking all around the house trying desperately to find another way to get inside when the doors were locked. And I found it!

On the back of the garage part of the house was the room where Mama had her washer and dryer. Since it was on the back of the garage, it was not officially a part of the house. That meant, I discovered, that the windows in that little room not only didn't lock, they didn't even have screens on them.

With a little bit of ingenuity, I soon perfected the new way in. Now, whenever I got home late, I could go around behind the garage end of the house, easily push up the window there, slide in on my stomach over the washing machine, close the window, creep in through the garage, slip in the kitchen door from the garage—all without waking my mama! It was a great plan, and it always worked perfectly!

I didn't tell my brother Joe about my secret entrance. *After all,* I thought, *someone needs to get caught!* Mama would be so disappointed otherwise.

As it turned out, it was more than thirty-five years before I ever told my brother about coming in over the washing machine. Our mother was in the nursing home in what would turn out to be the final months of her life. One day my brother and I went to visit her, and when we got to her room, she was stretched out on her back on top of her made-up bed. Her eyes were closed. Her breathing sounded slow and measured. We did not bother her. Joe and I simply sat down, and the two of us started visiting. As usual, our talk turned to remembering.

"Remember when we turned the swingset over?" Joe said. "I wouldn't have told," he said, "because I was certain that I had done something to make it turn over." We laughed, both of us realizing that whenever trouble came, we had each one assumed that we were individually to blame.

Then it was my turn. "Remember," I started, "when we

were in high school and Mama would lock us out when we stayed out too late at night?"

"Yeah," he remembered. "Then she would be waiting in the kitchen when she heard that big garage door open."

I continued my version of the story. "Well," I lingered over the words, "I found another way to get in." Then, thirty-five years later, I told him the whole story of how I climbed in through the back window and left him to be the one who got caught.

He listened, smiling all of the time. Then he said, "I never found that window you used. I came in another way. Remember that little glassed-in porch on the back of the living room? Those windows cranked out, you know. You could go in there in the daytime and slip the crank bar out of its track and then just pull the window open from the outside. It helped if you put a bucket in the bushes so you had something to stand on. You could reach the window better that way. After I found that window, I didn't get caught again either. I thought I was keeping it a secret from you!"

We both laughed.

Suddenly, without even the courtesy of opening her eyes, Mama stretched on the bed and spoke. "I knew that," was all that she said.

Joe and I turned to her. "You knew what?" we asked in unison.

"I knew all of that. I knew all about the laundry room and all about the back porch also. I knew you were going to do it!"

Without thinking, I asked, "How did you know?"

Suddenly I realized that it was a silly question. I already knew her answer. "I knew," she smiled, "because that's what boys do. You were both too smart to keep on getting caught over and over again."

"Well"—it was Joe this time who asked—"if you were so smart, why didn't you catch us?"

Mama was really smiling now, her eyes were still closed. "Why would I have wanted to catch you and have to start getting up again at night? You boys had it all fixed for me. I not only knew that you were home, I knew which one of you was home at what time. I knew who came in over the washing machine and who came in by the glassed-in porch. All I had to do was listen. Then, when I had heard both of you, I could say to myself, *They're home now. We can all go to sleep.*"

This time it was Joe who asked, "How did you know to do that?"

"Because," she answered, "that's what Mamas do!"

It was only a few months after that when Mama died.

When she died, Joe and I thought that we would never again hear the sound of her voice. We were wrong! We hear her all of the time.

I think she shows up every time one of us does one of those things "boys do." At least that's when I hear her voice.

Sometimes she says, "You'd better put that back!" Lots of times she says, "I'll bet you won't do that again!" And once in a while she says, "You're home now. We can all go to sleep."

PEAS AND CARROTS

At the little house on Plott Creek, we lived in the kitchen. The kitchen had the wood stove where Mama cooked, so it was the warmest room in the house in the wintertime. Daddy always said that you didn't want heat in the bedrooms because you were supposed to go to sleep when you went in the bedroom, and a warm bedroom would make you stay up and play instead of going to sleep.

Even in the summertime, because it was our habit, we lived in the kitchen.

In the kitchen we had a white wooden table with four wooden chairs. That is where we ate. Everybody always sat at the same places. Daddy sat in the corner behind the table, where he could not possibly get out to help my mama. I sat on the back side against the wall so that nothing or nobody could sneak up behind me and get me. Joe sat on the outside because he wasn't scared that anybody was going to get him.

Mama didn't sit. Mama stood between the table and the stove, where she nibbled while she watched the stove, monitored the plates, and brought more food whenever she (on her own) decided that someone needed more.

"Lucille, sit down and eat," Daddy would say.

"I ate while I was cooking!" was always her answer.

"Lucille, sit down and eat," he would repeat.

"I'll eat when everybody else gets finished," she would respond. I do not ever remember our mama sitting down at the table during a meal.

There was one big rule about food: "You don't waste food!" It was Mama's rule. Having grown up on a farm with eight siblings during the Great Depression, Mama never thought there was going to be enough food for tomorrow, so the rule was firm and fast.

It would not have been a bad rule if we had been allowed to serve our own plates. But it didn't work that way.

Mama would come to the table, pick up each of the plates in turn, take them to the stove, and serve what she decided you needed to eat. She would dish up potatoes ("to be big and strong"), meat ("so your blood will be good and red"), greens ("so you can run fast"), and so on, until the plate was mounded and you had to sit there for some good time trying to figure out how to make the food disappear.

One day Joe looked up at Daddy and asked, "Is there anything that you can do with food except eat it?"

Daddy answered, "Maybe so—but then you couldn't call it food."

That same kitchen table was also where we played. Joe and I would drape a blanket over the table and it would become a cave under there, we would drape a blanket over the table and it would become a log cabin under there, we would drape a blanket over the table and it would become a tepee under there, we would drape a blanket—we were not very creative. This game was all that we knew to do.

One afternoon when Mama was not in the room, Joe and I were playing under the kitchen table, and we got to kicking and rolling around. Since she was not there to stop us, we knew that it was safe to fight! We got a little too rough, and one of us kicked and broke one of the corner legs right off of the table. It was certain that we were in big trouble!

I hurried to tell Mama so that I could get there first and say, "Joe just broke the table!"

But there was no trouble at all. Mama calmly said, "Oh, boy! At last we can get a new table!"

My only thought was, *Why didn't you tell us you wanted a new table? We could have broken this one at any time!*

So we dispatched the broken table to the garage and went

to the furniture store in town for Mama to pick out the new table. She was so excited. Daddy told her to get whatever she wanted, and she picked out what the store man called "a dinette set."

The top of the new table was a beautiful gray Formica that looked like plastic marble. The corners of the table were not square; they were gently rounded, and the sides and ends of the table actually dipped in a little bit. The legs were like silvery chrome pipes, two on each corner, that started out of sight up under the corners of the table and, as they curved down into sight, joined in a pair that ended with little plastic feet where they met the floor.

On the chairs, the chrome pipes ran from the backs down beside the seats and ended in an unbroken curve where they settled on the floor. Joe and I soon learned that we could grab hold of the sides of the seats so that we didn't fall out, then bounce up and down and travel all over the room.

One day we were sitting at the new table eating supper. I was seven years old and Joe was five. Mama had included in this particular meal my least favorite food: canned mixed peas and carrots. I hated mixed peas and carrots. The little peas had been cooked and canned so long that they were not nice and round anymore but rather squatted on the plate and bulged out on the sides. They also were not bright and fresh green anymore but had cooked down to the faded color of monkey vomit. The poor little cubic carrots were so ashamed of being called carrots that they sucked in on the sides and turned gray on the corners. Besides this, the mixed peas and carrots lived in runny, greenish-grayish juice that ran out, soaked your bread, and ruined all your other food. I hated peas and carrots.

Mama would say, "You have to eat your peas and carrots or you can't see in the dark." I would think, *You don't let me stay up in the dark to begin with! So I don't need to eat peas and carrots.*

I was doing the best I could. I had already eaten everything else. Compared to the peas and carrots, everything else was good!

I had carefully lined up the peas and carrots right around the rim of the plate. This was so that if any of them wanted to jump off and kill themselves, they would be right up there ready to do it. I had counted them: seventy-four. That's how many I had to get rid of.

I was just biding my time at the table, looking at the peas and carrots and feeling around under the new table with my hands. Even now I remember what your hands are like when you are about seven years old. It was just like when my hands took the newspaper out of the Mehaffeys' mailbox: I did not personally do it. Kids are not personally responsible for their hands. (Some people have hands like that all of their lives!)

All of a sudden one of my hands found the end of one of the pipes that curved down to make the table legs. The end of the pipe was open, and it was hollow. All of a sudden my fingers realized: *You could put something in there.*

The next time Mama turned around to the stove, one of my hands came up on top of the table, picked up some peas and carrots, and traveled back under the table. It was easy. The peas and carrots went right into the hollow-pipe table leg! As far as your finger could reach you could push them right on back in there, and then there was room for more. I kept loading and pushing until all of the peas and carrots had been moved from my plate to the table leg.

That first night, I put seventy-four peas and carrots in the table leg, but that was just the beginning. From then on, I loved peas and carrots. They were the most fun of any food we ever had.

I put all of my peas and carrots in the table leg every time we had them the year that I was seven years old. I put peas and carrots in the table leg the entire year that I was eight years old. I put peas and carrots in the table leg the whole year that I was nine years old.

When I was ten years old, I had to swap sides of the table

with my brother. I had filled up the four legs on my side of the table, and I needed to start on his! Once on the other side, I continued putting peas and carrots in the new table legs the entire year that I was eleven years old. I would still be putting peas and carrots in the table leg, but when I was twelve years old, we moved to a new house.

The day of the move, Daddy and my Uncle Spencer were loading things into Uncle Spencer's pickup truck. They were trying to get everything from the kitchen to fit in one truck-load. All of a sudden Uncle Spencer said to Daddy, "Joe . . . I think that if we would turn this table upside down and take off the legs, we could get it to fit a lot better."

I thought, *Oh, no!*

They picked up the table and turned it over. At first nothing happened, but when they put it down—*thunk*—upside down on the floor, a sound went *rattle-rattle-rattle-rattle,* up inside the legs, and as the sound came down the legs, out came years of dried-up peas and carrots into little piles on the upside-down tabletop.

Mama was watching them work. When she saw the piles of peas and carrots, her eyes bulged out. "We don't waste food!" she said. "Now, you go and find a container and put that food in it, and we will take it to our new house until we figure out what to do with it."

So when we unpacked at the new house, along with our toys, books, and furniture, there was a big wide-mouthed canning jar filled to the brim with antique peas and carrots. Mama kept them on a shelf in the kitchen. Once in a while she would come in the kitchen and say, "Oh, what should we have for supper tonight?" She would pick up the jar of peas and carrots and say, "Maybe we should have some of these!" then put the jar back on the shelf and mutter, "No, maybe we should wait a little bit longer."

It had been the very beginning of the summer when we moved to the new house. Later on that summer, the Methodist church had a week-long program called "Vacation Bible School for Children." Joe and I both went for the whole week.

At Vacation Bible School, we had little classes for every age level. In our classes we learned songs and games, and each day we had what the teachers called "Arts and Crafts."

Joe's class was making things like baskets and boxes by gluing together old Popsicle sticks that had been bleached with Clorox. One of the classes made pottery on a little wheel that belonged to one of the teachers. In still another class, all of the students were making hand-woven wall hangings. In my class, we were to make what our teacher called mosaic pictures.

The teacher explained that mosaic pictures were an old

kind of artwork that went way back to Bible times, when people did not even know what paint was. You didn't paint the pictures. No, you made mosaic pictures by gluing things onto the background surface.

We started by taking white boards and choosing a picture we wanted to make. All of the pictures came out of Bible stories, and most of them were animals. I chose a big rooster. It was supposed to be the one that crowed when Peter told a lie.

We traced the pictures onto the white board very carefully, and then our teacher helped us plan what came next.

"This is what you do," she said. "You take small objects that are the right colors, then you glue them onto the background to make the picture." She had some buttons and some popcorn and some macaroni, and without gluing them down, she showed us ways to arrange these things to make a picture.

Then our teacher gave us the next instructions: "Now, all of you go home and look all around your house and see if you can find anything you can bring back tomorrow to use in your picture or to share with others. If everyone brings one or two things, and brings enough to share, then you will have lots of colors and textures to work with."

Before we even got home that day, I already knew what I was going to do. I remembered the day when my brother Joe had asked Daddy, "Is there anything you can do with food except eat it?" I also remembered that Daddy had said, "Maybe so—but then you couldn't call it food." *Of course not,* I thought. *You call it Art Supplies!*

The next morning I got up early, slipped into the kitchen, and took the jar of dried peas and carrots down from the shelf. I slipped them into the bag with my lunch and the other things I needed for the day at Bible School. When Mama saw how big the bag was, she said, "What are you taking to Bible School today?"

"Art supplies!" was all I said.

When I got to Bible School that day, I had so many dried peas and carrots that there were enough to share with everybody. And everybody shared what they had brought with me.

The rooster turned out to be very beautiful. I knew from our roosters at home that its tail needed to be really colorful, and it was: it was striped in green and yellow and outlined in macaroni one of the other kids had shared with me!

On Sunday, after Vacation Bible School was all over, all the adults were invited to visit our classrooms after church so they could see what we had done during the week. After the little show time, we could then take our work home with us. Of course, Mama and Daddy came down to see what Joe and I had done.

Mama looked at all of the things all of the classes had done. "Oh, look!" she started, "This class made baskets out of Popsicle sticks. How interesting. Oh, look at this. This class used a real wheel to make pottery! I bet that was fun." We kept on going from class to class. "Will you look at this? This class did some hand weaving and made wall decorations! Isn't that beautiful?" We were now coming to my classroom.

"*Ohhh!*" Mama cried out. When I heard that sound, I knew that she had seen the rooster! I already knew what she was going to say next: "We don't waste food!"

Daddy laughed. "Lighten up, Lucille!" he offered. "That's not food . . . that's what you call *art!*" Mama then got so tickled that I didn't even get into trouble. For many years after that, the pea-and-carrot rooster decorated the end wall in our kitchen, until some little insects that didn't know the difference between food and art started to eat it and we had to throw it away.

JACK MARR BUILDS A HOUSE

After my parents married in 1943, they bought the corner of a farm about two miles outside of Sulpher Springs. That meant they could have a large garden, a milk cow, chickens for eggs and meat, a pig, and a lot of apple trees so that we would not starve to death in case the bank closed. After all, Mr. Roosevelt was not the president anymore (even though his framed picture hung on our kitchen wall on through Mr. Eisenhower's presidency) and if the Depression came back, who knew what might happen?

Our little six-acre farm, which seemed completely rural as it was surrounded by active farmland, was a long strip that ran between Plott Creek at its back edge and Plott Creek Road at its front. At its widest end, the creek was about five hundred feet back from the road, and as you moved toward town, the creek and the road got closer and closer together until our land ended with the road and creek being side by side.

Our house sat near the center of this plot, with the garden above it, chickens and pig behind it, and cow pasture narrowing below it. Where the land narrowed until the creek and road were only about a hundred feet apart, my daddy fenced it across and let the bottom triangle grow up with briars and bushes. Before the fence, that corner had been the frequently used exit for our cow, Helen, when she wanted to get out.

As years passed and that corner grew up more and more, Daddy was often heard to say that it was "good for nothing." This assessment must have gotten around town, because one day something happened that would never have come to pass unless he had been overheard.

That day, we heard a knock at the door of our house. When we went to the door, there on the porch stood a young man and a woman. Their names were Jack and Ida Marr, and they were newly married.

"Mr. Davis," Jack Marr said to my daddy, "I've heard that that little corner of land down below your cow barn isn't worth anything." Daddy just stood there waiting to see what was coming next. "Since you've said it's not worth anything and you own it, we were wondering if you might let us have it at a good price so we could build a house on it."

In that moment, my daddy discovered that the land was, in fact, worth something! Someone wanted to buy it. He and the Marrs had a little meeting at the kitchen table, and sure enough, a deal was made for them to buy the land. Mama even allowed as how it would be a good thing to have that land cleaned up and get some neighbors at the same time.

I was eleven years old at this time, and this proved to be the beginning of one of the most educational periods of time in my young life. As it turned out, Jack Marr planned to build his own house, and since I was there, I was to be his volunteer helper every step of the way—whether he needed me or not!

Jack Marr worked the first shift at Dayton Rubber Company, and he got off of work at three o'clock in the afternoon. I got home from school at about the same time, so when he got there, I was ready and waiting. From foundations to ceilings, I watched and helped every step of the way.

My vocabulary improved as I helped Jack Marr work on the new house. I learned words like *soffit* and *batter-board* and *sleeper,* as well as a lot of little short words that Jack Marr sometimes used when he needed to make something fit or— more often—when he missed a nail and hit some part of his body instead. I loved watching him work and thinking that I was doing something worthwhile.

There was only one problem about Jack Marr building the new house: he worked on it on Sundays!

At our house we got up on Sunday mornings to a once-a-week breakfast of hotcakes while Daddy read the funny papers to us from the Asheville *Citizen-Times*. As soon as breakfast was finished, Joe and I hurried to get dressed so our whole family could go to Sunday school and church at the Methodist church in town. You had to be pretty sick to get out of going to Sunday school, even more so than church.

All dressed up, we would get into our Plymouth, and Daddy would pull out into Plott Creek Road and turn left toward town. As soon as we started down the gravel road, Mama was already looking. Her eyes focused toward the new Jack Marr house site and darted back and forth searching for evidence of activity there. As soon as she would see Jack, her eyes would stop with a locked-on stare, which followed him as her head turned while our car passed by and went on out of sight.

Then Mama would turn to Daddy and say, "That man doesn't go to church!" Then she would pause for the pronouncement to settle in, like it was somehow Daddy's fault for selling the Marrs the land to begin with.

As soon as we got home from church that first Sunday, I lingered in the kitchen until Mama busied herself with Sunday dinner preparations, then I slipped out the door and hurried across the cow pasture looking for Jack Marr. My mission was to find him so that I could tell him what my mother had said about him. I was beginning to discover that whenever Mama talked about people, if I would tell them what she had to say, I would often hear two stories instead of just the one she had told to begin with.

"Jack," I began, "my mama says that you don't go to church!" Then I waited for his reply.

Jack Marr stopped planing on the piece of wood he had been shaping. He came over to where I was without saying anything. All of a sudden I began to wonder whether I should have come over here to tell him this or not. He sat down on a pile of lumber and he motioned me to sit down beside him.

"Son," he said, "I have to get this house in the dry before wintertime, no matter what I would rather be doing on Sundays. But besides that, let me tell you something. Church is not somewhere you go."

"It's not?" I must have looked amazed at age eleven. "We go!"

"No," Jack Marr went on. "Church is what happens wherever you are when everybody you meet has a better day because they met you than they could have had if they hadn't met you at all. That is a whole lot harder than just going somewhere for an hour on Sunday."

I thought about that, and the only thing I could make out

of it was that maybe what Jack Marr had said could get me out of going to Methodist Sunday school. So I went home and told my mama all about it. She was not impressed, and the next Sunday I had to go back to Sunday school like always.

As the fall of the year went on, Jack Marr, with my after-school and Saturday help, continued working on the new house. About the end of October, it was finally finished enough on the inside for the Marrs to move in. Ida Marr told my mama, "If we can just get in before cold weather, then Jack and I can both work on the rest of the outside whenever we have pretty weather."

On the first Saturday after the Marrs moved into their new house, they walked over across our pasture in the early after-noon and invited us to come over and have supper with them that night. We promised that we would, and about six o'clock we walked across from our side of the pasture, wiggled through the barbed-wire pasture fence (with Daddy promis-ing that he would put in a gate now that we had neighbors), and walked on boards across the unleveled raw dirt that would later be a yard.

The Marrs had an electric doorbell, the first one that I had ever seen. Daddy had to be the one to push the button. From inside the house we heard, *Ding-dong-ding-dong. Ding-dong-*

ding-dong. We could hear footsteps as Ida Marr came to the door, opened it, and ushered all of us inside.

We ate with them in their new kitchen, after they apologized that the dining room wasn't furnished yet. After supper was over, Ida turned down Mama's offer to help with the dishes, then proceeded to show all of us how she rinsed the dishes and then put them into a top-loading General Electric dishwasher, again the first one we had ever seen.

The dishwasher sounded like a rainstorm with a heavy wind. Once Ida had it started, she ushered us into the living room and seated us. Jack Marr walked over to a brand new television set and actually turned it on! After a few pops and flashes, a snowy picture came on the screen, and our family was watching the first television set that we had ever seen that was turned on! We had looked at a television set in the furniture store in town before, but they never turned them on in the furniture store. Daddy said that it was because no one would want to buy a television set that had some of the programs already used up on it.

There, before our wondering eyes, in living black and white, we saw Red Foley from Renfro Valley, Kentucky. Red Foley, whom I would later come to know as Pat Boone's father-in-law, was singing a wonderful song called "The Salty

Dog Rag." When the *Renfro Valley* show was finished, we watched a program called *Lawrence Welk,* with bubbles rising up in the air and Daddy telling us who each of the musicians in the Lawrence Welk band looked like to him! It was an evening of wonder! At last we had to go home, because Mama reminded us out loud that tomorrow was Sunday and that we had to get up and go to Sunday school.

On Sunday morning we got up to our usual pancake breakfast, after which we were soon ready to go to the Methodist church. I already knew what Mama was going to do even before we turned left out of the driveway. "We did have a good time over there with them last night," she started, "But . . . that Jack still doesn't go to church."

Since the inside of the house was finished now, Jack Marr really was down to the last bit of finish work on the outside. As we drove down the road and watched him that morning, he was painting the wood trim around and under the eaves of the house. Jack was up near the top of a tall A-frame ladder. He had a bucket of white paint on the fold-out bucket step and we watched as he dipped the brush in the bucket, then reached out to paint back and forth along the soffit.

When Sunday school and church were over, we got in the car and returned home.

As Daddy turned into our driveway, I could look over and

see that Jack Marr had finished painting along the front side of the house and was now on the ladder painting the eaves along the end of the house toward our cow pasture.

Mama went into the kitchen to finish the dinner she had started that morning, and I headed out the door and across the pasture to visit with Jack until our food was ready.

As I crossed the pasture, I could see Jack, there on the top of the A-frame ladder. He was painting back and forth, back and forth, in long, beautiful, even strokes of the brush. As I got closer to the Marrs' house, I could begin to hear that Jack was painting to music. Out through the open door and out of the open window came the most beautiful music I had ever heard. It was something like the music we heard in church each Sunday but much more beautiful. I stopped for a moment and just listened and watched as the music flowed out of the window, and in perfect time, the paint flowed from Jack Marr's brush and along the long eaves of the house.

When I got near their house, Ida came to the back door and motioned to me. I met her at the screen door and followed her inside. Without a word, she led me through the kitchen and on into the living room. The big television set was turned on, and from it was coming that beautiful music by which Jack Marr was painting. It was—from Salt Lake City, Utah—the Mormon Tabernacle Choir.

Ida and I stood there, side by side, as we watched and listened to the choir. As we listened, I would look back and forth between the television and the living room window, through which I could watch Jack, still at the very top of the ladder, as he rhythmically painted to the beauty of the tabernacle music. The whole experience was one of joy!

Finally the television broadcast came to an end and the music stopped. I watched Jack continue painting as the announcer came on and said, "This program has been brought to you by the Church of Jesus Christ of Ladder-Day Saints."

That's when I knew what Jack Marr was! He was one of those Ladder-Day Saints, and everything that he had said to me about church made sense.

What I had just seen and heard made me feel good. I had had a better day because I had heard the music and watched his good work than I could ever have had if I had seen and heard none of it. Church isn't a place you go . . . it is, like he said, what happens when you work to make everyone you meet have a better day because they met you than they could have had if they hadn't met you.

Years later, in Utah, when I began to meet the real Latter-Day Saints, I realized that I was not as far off as I might have imagined. The real ones I know do work to make your day better in their presence that it would have been had you never met them.

FRUITCAKE COOKIES

Mama became a second-grade teacher the same year I was in the second grade. She had taught school before she and Daddy got married but had taken time off while Joe and I were babies. When she started back to teaching, I was scared to death that I would end up in her room at school. But I was safe!

It seemed quite annoying at first to have to go to the same school where your own mother was one of the teachers. At times I completely hated it. But by the time that year was over, I had discovered two times of the year when it was a wonderful thing to have a schoolteacher for a mother.

One of those two days was the day when school got out for the summer. On that day Mama cleaned out her classroom at school. Along with all of the "teacher things" that she brought home to work on for the summer, she also brought a big box. In this box were all of the things that she had taken away from children all through the course of the year. She gave the box of goodies to me and my brother, Joe, and we had enough new toys to keep us happy throughout the entire course of the summer.

That wonderful box held yo-yos and slingshots. We got paddles with rubber balls on rubber bands that were supposed to "fly back" if you hit them the right way. We found cap pistols and enough water pistols to supply all of the cousins and neighbors put together. We even found an old cheap knife.

Actually, the end-of-school treasure was the second time that year that I had been glad my mama was a schoolteacher. The first great time had been the day school got out for Christmas.

In those days it was common for students to give their teachers Christmas presents. Half of the presents (I think they came from the girls) were terrible-smelling bottles of dime-store perfume with some name like "Flowers of the Nile." They smelled like flowers from the funeral of someone who had died a long time ago. Mama would not dare use any of that perfume. She said that if you ever got that smell on you, it would never come off!

The other half of the presents (I knew these came from the boys) were boxes of cheap chocolate-covered cherries. Mama didn't like chocolate-covered cherries, so my brother and I eventually ended up with enough candy to last us until springtime.

Almost all the children in Sulpher Springs gave Christmas presents to their teachers. I was sure that Lynn Conard had to spend two years in the second grade, not because he couldn't pass his work but rather because he didn't give Miss Lois Harrold a Christmas present. Joe and I always gave our teachers presents on the day that school got out for Christmas.

Because Mama always got perfume and candy, which she did appreciate "in thought if not in deed," she wanted to be sure that when Joe and I gave presents to our teachers they were more appropriate and more appreciated than perfume and candy.

Being a wonderful cook, Mama's natural decision was to bake something that our teachers would not only appreciate but that would be helpful to them during the holiday season. One year it was moist, buttermilk layer cake with freshly grated coconut on top. Another year it was mint-flavored Chocolate Midnight Delight cake. Still another Christmas she made wonderful-smelling seven-layer spice cakes with caramel icing.

Mama always made three cakes. There was one for my teacher, one for Joe's teacher, and an extra one for us to keep at home, partly so we could enjoy it and partly so that she could test it and decide whether the ones we had given to our teachers had been "fit to eat."

Problems began to arise when I got to junior high school.

I now had three teachers, and with a cake for each one of them, plus one for my brother's teacher and one for us to keep at home, Mama was baking and decorating five cakes during the week that school got out for Christmas.

She managed this well for the two years that I was in junior high school. Then suddenly, the entire world changed. I entered high school as a ninth-grader, and Joe entered junior high as a seventh-grader. Suddenly Mama realized that, between the two of us, we had a total of nine teachers! I can still see the expression on her face as she worked solidly from Friday afternoon until Sunday night to bake ten pound cakes the weekend before school got out for Christmas. Luckily for the world not a single one of them fell.

On the day that we took the cakes to school, Mama announced, "Next year we are not going to do this!"

Every single teacher that I had that year wrote *me* a personal thank-you note for the delicious pound cakes!

It was not until Thanksgiving the next year that Mama brought up the Christmas present issue again. "You have six teachers again this year," she started, "and your brother has three. In one more year, you will have six teachers each. I just cannot keep on making all of these cakes!"

She went on, "I have an idea. There is a wonderful and beautiful book at the bookstore called *Christmas Ideals*. It is filled with poems and stories about Christmas. I think that it would be a nice thing to give each one of your teachers a book for Christmas. What do you think about that?"

Joe didn't say anything. I thought that giving a teacher another book was about the dumbest thing that I had ever heard. I knew that I did not have one single teacher who wanted to eat a book! They wanted food, and I knew that! My grades needed help, and only sugar would do the trick. I searched my brain for another idea as fast as I could.

Mama and her friends were always swapping the latest in fashionable recipes, and earlier in the fall of the year, the newest popular recipe was one for "Coca-Cola Fruitcake Cookies." The cookies did not either look or taste like the name *fruitcake* sounded. They were not at all like the usual doorstop fruitcakes we often got for Christmas. No, these cookies were delicious.

The light batter was made with bubbly Coca-Cola instead of milk, and the cookies were filled with candied cherries and all sorts of other fruits and nuts. Mama had tried the recipe out by making a lot of them for Halloween trick-or-treats, and we had had plenty left over to eat. I knew that she was planning to make them again for Christmas, and I knew that the group of teachers that I had this year would really love them!

"I have a better idea, Mama," I started my pitch. "Remember

those great fruitcake cookies that you made for Halloween? They were so good, and they didn't seem to be real hard for you to make. They were about the best cookies that I have ever had. I know that it would be a lot of work, but what I really wish is that my teachers could taste how great those cookies were. If I help you, is it possible that we might make a batch of those cookies big enough to divide up among all my teachers for Christmas? These high school teachers are discriminating, and I know they would like that a lot better than getting another book."

Mama just sighed. I knew she could not resist the temptation to show off her baking skills. "You'll have to help a lot," she said, "and we will have to make them over the Thanksgiving holidays. They are not really good when you first bake them. They have to be sealed up so that they can mellow for a couple of weeks until they get good and soft and all of the flavors blend together. Do you want to try that?"

The plan was made. I knew that my grades would go up for sure when my teachers got the cookies and the sugared contents did their magic. All during the Thanksgiving holidays, our whole family baked cookies. We must have had five hundred cookies by the time Mama decided that we probably had enough.

While all of the baking was going on, Mama had sent me

out to the storage room behind the garage where we kept all of the things that we didn't-need-right-now-but-might-need-someday. Along with several dozen hospital bud-vases, years of folded and saved grocery bags, and every piece of Tupperware ever made that had a missing lid, I found an accumulation of cake tins that had gathered themselves and reproduced in the dark over a period of years. My job was to pick out the nine "biggest and best"—six for my teachers, three for Joe's teachers. The rest of the cookies, those for our family to eat, would go into a huge Tupperware cake box that would hold as much as any three of the tins put together.

We washed and dried the cookie tins, lined them with red and green tissue paper, filled each one with as many freshly-baked fruitcake cookies as would fit inside, and put on the tight lids so that the cookies would "mellow" for the coming weeks and be ready when school got out for Christmas.

As we stacked up the filled tins, Mama noticed that they did not all "look like Christmas," as she said. Some of them had flowers on the lids, some of them had animal pictures on the lids, one had a Scotch plaid pattern, and one even had autumn leaves decorating its cover. "We need to make these cookie tins look like Christmas," she said.

Mama then proceeded to find some old Christmas cards. Carefully, she cut out the pictures on the front panels. She gave me the pictures, along with some wide red and green ribbon, and told me to decorate the cookie tins so that they would "look like Christmas." I got to work and did a beautiful job.

Three weeks passed, and finally the last day of school arrived. That day I started to school with six tins of cookies, confident that they would be the best-loved gifts these particular teachers ever received.

First period of the day, the first tin of cookies went to Miss McClure, my Latin teacher. "Surprise!" I said. "Don't open it until you get home!"

All through the day I distributed cookies. A tin each went to Mrs. Williams, my history teacher, to Miss Reed in geometry, to Mr. Crocker in the band building, to chemistry's Mr. Huffaker, and to little Miss Terrell in English. They all thanked me, especially Miss Terrell, who told me that her father, who lived with her, loved cookies and that my present would make their whole holiday season better than ever.

I went home that day with the knowledge that my grades would improve dramatically and that I would enjoy profuse thanks and high praise when we returned to school. At home, we enjoyed our own allotment of fruitcake cookies all through the holidays.

As the end of the holiday break drew near, I actually began to look forward to returning to school. I was certain that everyone in my classes would hear about the wonderful cookies on our first day back at school.

On the morning of the first day back at school, I walked into Miss McClure's Latin class and saw that Miss McClure was not there. Instead, at the head of the class stood Miss Kellett, whom I knew to be an ancient retired Latin teacher from another era. "Come in, boys and girls," Miss Kellett warbled. "I am going to be your substitute teacher today. You see, Miss McClure is sick! I understand that it could be a few days before she is able to come back."

Second period was history with Mrs. Williams. Unlike Miss Kellett, I did not know the strange woman who was waiting for us in Mrs. Williams's class. "I am your substitute," she introduced herself. "Mrs. Williams is sick! I will be with you until she returns."

My third-period class was geometry. Miss Reed, our teacher, was young and just out of college. She was waiting for us in the room when we entered. "Boys and girls"—she started the class almost before we were all seated—"work on these problems that I have written on the board. *I'll be right back!*" Miss Reed almost ran out of the room and into the teachers' lounge, which was located next door to the geometry room. Through the wall behind the blackboard we could hear a lot of flushing and running water.

When Miss Reed came back, she didn't even seem interested in the work that we had done. She quickly erased the old problems and wrote a new set on the board, pointed to the new problems, and said, "Now do these . . . *I'll be right back!"*

Miss Reed made six trips out of the classroom during a fifty-minute class period, and at the end of the class period, she didn't even remember to take up all the work we had done.

Fourth period was normal. Mr. Crocker, our band director, was just fine. We had our usual band class and then went to lunch.

After lunch, everything fell apart again. We had a substitute teacher for Mr. Huffaker in chemistry class, and, last period of the day, there was a substitute for little Miss Terrell, our English teacher.

When school got out, I waited for Mama to come and pick me up after she finished at her school. It was usually about a twenty-minute wait, and my normal waiting place was the front steps of the band building. Even in the wintertime, the afternoon sun and the building's shelter from the wind kept it warmer there than anywhere else.

I was sitting on the band building steps, waiting, when Mr. Crocker, my band director, came out and spoke to me. "I need to talk with you," he said, and he led me inside the building and into his office.

Once inside, Mr. Crocker sat behind his desk and motioned me to a chair on the other side. This had to be serious since he almost never actually used his desk. He had already closed the door when we came into the room so no one else could hear our conversation.

"I know you wouldn't do anything like this," Mr. Crocker said slowly and seriously, "but . . . is there any chance that you might have put something in those cookies you gave me for Christmas? I ate the first one, and all of a sudden, I got so dizzy that I could hardly get to the bathroom to throw up. I was scared to eat any more of them after that."

Suddenly, I had a religious experience! It was just like St. Paul in the book of Acts where he has been blind and then gets his sight back. It says, "Something like scales fell from his eyes." Like St. Paul, I could see every single thing that had happened from Thanksgiving to this moment.

It started when we had baked the cookies at Thanksgiving time and had filled the tins. Mama had given me the Christmas card pictures and the ribbons and had told me to "make the tins look like Christmas." I had decided to fasten pictures to both the outside and inside surfaces of the lids so that when my teachers took off the lids, a Christmas scene would be waiting there.

It was hard to stick the paper pictures to the metal lids, but

I knew what to do—I built model airplanes! So, armed with a big tube of model airplane glue, I had squirted a big glob of the volatile cement all over the inside of the lid, stuck on the pictures, and put the lids back on the cookies. The fruitcake cookies had then sat there *sniffing glue* for three weeks!

"No," I said, with true innocence, "I didn't put anything in those cookies. My mama made them."

"I didn't think you would have," he said. Then he looked away as he mused to himself, "It really must have been a little case of the flu. I heard that a whole bunch of teachers are out sick today. Doesn't seem to have hit the kids yet, and they usually get it first. I guess I was lucky. I got over it in one day."

Slowly, through the course of the week, my teachers came back to school, one at a time. Little Miss Terrell didn't come back until the following Monday. She told us that her father had been sick too and that she had needed to be with him until he was all well and back to normal.

The next year, around Thanksgiving time, Mama brought up the topic of the teachers' Christmas presents. "It really wasn't so hard making all those cookies last year," she thought out loud. "You make them in batches and then you can pick the best ones to give away. Would you like to do that again? Except for Miss Terrell in English and Mr. Crocker in band, you have all different teachers this year. I'm sure that those two wouldn't mind getting some more cookies. You made those old tins look so pretty the way you decorated them!"

"Oh, Mama," I answered, "that's just too much work for you. It took us all of Thanksgiving for you to make all of those cookies. This year, why don't we give them a book? It will be easier for you!"

And so, we did give all of my teachers a new book for Christmas, and not a single one of them ever said one word about it! None, that is, except little Miss Terrell.

For two years I had mowed Miss Terrell's yard. The first time that spring that I went to mow, I finished and went to the door to get paid. Miss Terrell handed me the money, then said, "I never did thank you for that book you gave me for Christmas. I do love books. But I was secretly hoping that I might get some more of those wonderful cookies that you gave me the year before. They were so delicious, and they were such a comfort to my father and me while we were sick.

"Those cookies were so very good that we might have eaten them all on the first day," she went on, "but about the time we started on them, we both got sick—it was some kind of weird flu, I guess—and we were sick as could be for more than a week. Daddy and I just hoarded those cookies, and all the time that we were sick we ate one a day to cheer us up. They almost lasted until we started getting well!"

I did not say a single word, but I knew that a cookie refill might have killed the both of them!

If I had been raised Catholic, I would have been able to go to confession, tell the whole story, and unload it all. But being a simple guilty Methodist, all I could do was carry the weight of secrecy quietly for years.

The closest I managed to come to feeling better came the next time I went to mow Miss Terrell's yard. When I finished mowing, I slipped out of the back yard and went home without getting paid.

Later in the day, Miss Terrell called. "You didn't get paid," she said. "You need to come back so that you can get your money."

"Oh, no!" I answered, "No charge for today. You see, I was thinking about how disappointed you were when you didn't get cookies for Christmas, and I thought I would add mowing the yard today as a little late Christmas present! I am glad to do it!"

My senior year in high school I suggested that we give all of my teachers the cookbook that had the cookie recipe in it. "That way," I told Mama, "we have covered all of the bases."

We gave cookbooks with the cookie recipe especially marked, and I got six thank you notes . . . and I graduated.

A ROOM OF MY OWN

When I was nearly two-and-a-half years old, Mama told me that my Aunt Eddie was coming to our house for a few days and was going to bring my cousins, Andy and Kay, with her. The reason they were coming, Mama told me, was that she had to go somewhere for a few days and Aunt Eddie was going to take care of me during those days.

"Where do you have to go?" I remember asking in one way or another over and over again. Mama never did answer that question. She just said, "I won't be gone for very long. Aunt Eddie will stay with you and fix food for you and Daddy for all of your meals."

"So Daddy's not going to go with you?" I kept on asking questions.

"No, not for all of the time. He has to go to work. But he'll be home at night. Aunt Eddie will fix things that you like for both of you."

It was not that day, but about a week later, when suddenly,

Daddy drove Mama away in the car, and at the same time, Aunt Eddie arrived to take care of me.

That night Daddy was not at home for supper. He was still gone when Aunt Eddie put me to bed in my own room. "Which bed is yours?" she asked as she looked at the identical twin beds side by side in the room that we always called "my room."

"Both of them are my beds. This is my room," I insisted. "But I usually sleep in the bed over there beside the window. Bears sleep on the other bed."

It seemed to me that Mama was gone forever, though I later came to know that she was gone for exactly one week. Finally, one afternoon, Daddy came home early from the bank and led me to the front door of our house. "Let's both watch," he said. "They are bringing your mama home this afternoon."

I didn't know who "they" were, nor still where she had been. Daddy and I looked out the front-door window until a big, long, white car that was made like a station wagon backed into our driveway and then backed right across the grass almost to the steps of the front porch. The long white car had writing on the back, and it had a red light above the back door that was blinking on and off.

Two men got out of the car. They were dressed in white pants and white coats. They came around to the back of the big car and opened the door on the back. Then they pulled out a bed that had folded legs under it. The folded legs popped down to wheels at the bottom, and the men carried the bed up the steps and started to roll it into our house. All of a sudden I saw that it was my mama who was stretched out on the rolling bed. She smiled at me. On the foot of the rolling bed there was a big picnic basket with a handle curved over the top.

The two men rolled the bed into Mama and Daddy's bedroom and lifted her gently onto the big bed. As they did that, Daddy took the picnic basket, carried it into my bedroom, and put it on the second of my twin beds, the one where my bears usually slept. Then the two strange men left.

I went in to where Mama was so I could see her. She smiled at me. I said, "I thought you would never get back home. Where have you been?" She didn't answer the question.

"Go in there where your daddy put that basket and look and see what's in it," she directed me. Even in Mama and Daddy's bedroom, I could see through the door into my room and see the big basket. Without wondering or guessing, I walked into my room and over to the bed.

When I looked into the picnic basket, there was a baby in it! It was my new brother, Joe—the same name as my daddy. Without any conscious thought process in operation, I leaned over the basket and kissed my little brother! He was beautiful!

Years later I learned that, after having had difficulty in delivery when I was born, Mama had, for this baby, gone to the city of Asheville to have my brother by Caesarian. This was the reason that she had stayed for a week, and, having been an hour's drive from home, the reason that she came home in the ambulance instead of in Daddy's car.

From the first night that he was at home, my brother, Joe, slept in my room.

In the beginning, Joe kept sleeping in the picnic basket in which he rode home. The basket was on the other twin bed, just beside mine, with a pillow on either side of it so it couldn't wiggle off of the bed.

In no time, he outgrew the basket. Now Daddy made a little fence of slats that had side pieces that slid under the mattress to hold it in place. It made the twin bed into a sort of giant baby bed. Joe still slept beside me. There was a real down-through-the-family baby bed that was in the "guest bedroom," but since some other visiting family member like Aunt Laura or Aunt Mary or Grandmother Walker was so often there, the baby bed seemed to be used only for daytime naps. Joe slept in "my" room.

It was a good arrangement, the way God meant for it to be, and it worked for us. As time went on and we got older, sharing the room meant that there were two of us to argue with Mama about going to bed at night.

First I needed a drink of water, then he needed a drink of water, then I needed to go back to the bathroom, then he needed to go back to the bathroom, then it started all over again. Finally Mama would call Daddy for reinforcement, and we would lose the battle.

After the lights were out and our parents had left the room, Joe and I were there together to talk ourselves to sleep across from one another. It felt safe and right, and it lasted all through our preschool years and right on through elementary school. We got better at fighting with Mama about bedtime, though we always lost, and we still talked one another to sleep. It was good.

Then I turned thirteen! Overnight I had had enough of my brother. Overnight I had had enough of the whole family. (They were polite enough not to tell me what they all thought of me.) Overnight I knew that I needed—that I had to have—a room of my own.

"I want to move into the front bedroom," I announced to the entire family over supper a night or two later.

"You can't," Mama reasoned with me. "The front bedroom is the guest room. We have to have that room for when we have company."

"That was a long time ago," I argued back. "Aunt Laura used to stay there, but she died when I was five years old. Aunt Mary used to stay there when Uncle Gudger was in the army, but he came back and they have their own house. Besides, that was at our old house anyway. Grandmother Walker is about the only one who stays here, and she only stays about once a year when she gets sick. I can move out once a year if I need to!"

My argument got nowhere. We had to save the empty, unused, perfectly good bedroom for any relatives or company that happened to come by.

"Besides," Mama said, "you have a room. You have always had a room. It was your room before your brother was even born. It is a good room, and you need to stay in there so you can be close to your brother if he needs help in the night." It was the silliest argument I had ever heard. What could he need help doing? Sleeping?

That very Sunday at Sunday school, we had the most wonderful lesson we had ever had. When we got home for Sunday dinner, I could hardly wait to tell Mama what I had learned at Sunday school. "Guess what verse we learned today?" I eagerly asked.

"What?" Mama was so pleased that I was actually going to tell her voluntarily without being begged.

I was ready. In an extra loud voice I proclaimed, *"Am I my brother's keeper?"*

Mama was so mad after that that she couldn't even talk!

All through the fall and winter of that first teenage year, I shared the room with my brother in misery. I needed freedom, I needed responsibility, I needed privacy! I didn't get any of it.

The year before, I had joined the Boy Scouts. Since age eight I had been a Cub Scout, but at twelve, you got to become the real thing. I loved Boy Scouts. There were Boy Scout hikes and camping trips developing at the very same time that my buddy Davey Martin and I were beginning to go camping on our own, and one outdoor life complemented the other. It turned out to be Boy Scouts that provided me with my great escape route.

It was at the regular Tuesday night Boy Scout meeting in February that Mr. Todd, our Scoutmaster, made the announcement. "Listen up, boys"—this was the way he started everything he said to us—"I have here some applications for summer jobs at Camp Daniel Boone, our Boy Scout Camp. If any of you are interested in working at camp this summer, get one from me at the end of the meeting. For you younger boys there are some openings for junior staff positions that may not be for pay, but they will get you to camp for the whole summer."

This was a message from heaven! Without even having to think about it, I already knew what I was going to do. I would apply to get a job at Camp Daniel Boone for the summer, and

I would have ten full weeks away from my entire family! Ten weeks away from home would be almost as good as getting a room of my own.

When I got home from the meeting that night I announced the plan. To my surprise, there was no objection from either Daddy or Mama. Even Joe agreed that it would be a good thing for me to spend the summer working at the Scout camp. (Only later did it occur to me that they wanted a break from me as badly as I wanted one from them!) So I filled out the application.

There was a section of the form where you were to indicate "job preferences." You got to list three. My first choice was "canoe dock manager." I had never been in a canoe in my life and that sounded like great fun. My second choice was "archery range." I had always wanted to shoot bows and arrows, but Mama would not permit it. She insisted that I would "kill my brother." The third choice was working at the waterfront. My reasoning there was that, if I actually worked at the waterfront, maybe I would learn to swim.

At the bottom of the application form there was a short space where one of your parents was supposed to sign for their permission for you to work at camp. My parents were so supportive that they squeezed up their signatures so that both of them could sign on the same line!

I turned my application in at the next Scout meeting. I was actually the only person from my troop who applied for a job, but since my troop was not the only troop in town, there might be someone else whom I knew who could also be there for the summer with me.

Waiting for a reply seemed to go on forever, although it was only about three weeks later when the answer came. Mr. Todd handed me the envelope. It contained a letter of congratulations, acceptance to the Camp Daniel Boone staff of 1958, and a contract.

The contract said that I was being hired for a job called "kitchen steward." That sounded good to me. When I asked Daddy later on what that meant, he told me that it was a kind of assistant cook and that it would probably give me a lot of time off to do other things since you could only work in the kitchen at mealtimes. At the bottom of the contract was a space where the pay for the summer was indicated. The dollar sign had been marked out, and in its place was written the word EXPERIENCE. I did not care. I now had an escape route from my family for the summer.

I clearly remember the day that they all took me to camp. Mama had already packed up all the things that she decided I would need—sleeping bag, clothes, flashlight, canteen, first aid kit. Of all these things, the only thing I actually needed was my clothes. What I needed and didn't have were books—something to read, anything to read, any distraction would do before the summer was over.

Daddy took the afternoon off from work at the bank so we could all go to camp together. I had to arrive on a Friday afternoon because the first group of Boy Scouts was coming in on the following morning.

Joe's baby sleeping basket was now our official family picnic basket. Mama filled it with picnic food so that we could stop and have a picnic on the way to camp, even though it was only thirteen miles from home. I knew this exact distance because Daddy had told me, "Since you will only be thirteen miles away, it's almost like not leaving home. So we won't really need to come to see you during the summer. You will just barely be gone!" We did have the miserable family picnic on the way, and late on the first Friday afternoon in June, we arrived at Camp Daniel Boone.

Daddy gave me final instructions: "There is a telephone in the main lodge if you have a dire emergency. If you have a dire emergency, you can call us collect on that telephone—if you have a dire, extremely dire, emergency." I knew the meaning of this message. This message meant that I was not to make a telephone call for any reason for the entire duration of the summer.

After we unloaded my gear, I met the camp director, Mr. McPherson. I did not notice how fast my daddy drove away as the rest of the family left me, eager to get on with their own first summer of peaceful relief.

I had been in some hope that there might be someone else working at Camp Daniel Boone whom I already knew from home. As it turned out, there was someone there I knew and he ended up being my tentmate, but it was not as I had hoped it would be.

When tentmate assignments were made, I was to share a tent with a boy named Bobby Jensen. As he read the assignment, Mr. McPherson said, "The two of you are from the same place, and if you don't know one another already, then you should."

He didn't know that I knew Bobby Jensen better than I wanted to know him already.

Bobby Jensen had been in school with me since kindergarten. In kindergarten, he had been the world's worst bully and bad boy. In the eight years since that time, Bobby Jensen had gotten worse by the inch, worse by the pound. He and I had absolutely nothing in common except fear: he was scared of nothing, and I was scared of everything!

The two of us lived in a small army surplus tent that was pitched on a raised wooden tent platform. The tent had two army cot beds and a cabinet for our clothes and other belongings. The first problem was that the wooden floor was made of pine boards that had had big knots in them when they were new, but as they had dried out over the years, all of the knots had fallen out, leaving us with a floor scattered with knotholes that were exactly the right size for snakes to come through and up into our tent.

We would get into bed at night, and as soon as the lantern was blown out, Bobby Jensen would whisper, *"Rattle, rattle, rattle."* I would then be awake all night!

One of the first days we were there, I went to the infirmary and got a big roll of adhesive tape and taped up all of the snake holes in the floor. When Bobby Jensen saw what I had done, he said, "Now what did you go and do that for? Now all the snakes that come in to look around during in the day won't have any way to get back out!" I uncovered the holes immediately, and I quit sleeping again.

The job of kitchen steward did not really involve cooking. It involved going to the kitchen by six in the morning to fetch and carry everything Mrs. Deerbone, the cook, needed, and washing pots and pans as she finished with them. It involved setting up the food line and trying to supervise the assigned Scouts as they served one another, and again as they were on duty to wash all the dishes when the meal was over. They were so hard to manage that I ended up doing most of the dish-washing over or just doing it myself to begin with. About the time I had them working together, the week would be over and another fresh bunch would come in.

The job was extra problematic because Bobby Jensen was the other kitchen steward. Bobby did not like to get up early, so the dilemma was to either put up with his troublemaking, or leave him asleep and do double duty. I ended up much hap-pier doing work for us both than dealing with his presence.

Perhaps the biggest surprise of the job was how long it took to deal with each meal. The reporting time for breakfast was six o'clock in the morning. That's when we started to get ready for the meal that was served at seven-thirty. On the very first morning I was there, Mrs. Deerbone had me crack thirty dozen small, cold-storage, army-surplus eggs into a big pot. Bobby Jensen finally showed up for work just as I was finished and my fingers were frozen.

As the day went on, I learned the schedule. By the time everything was all cleaned up—floors swept and dishes washed—it would be nine-thirty. Reporting time for lunch duty was ten-thirty, and by the time all the same work was done over again, it was two o'clock. Supper duty started at four o'clock, so I had a break of about two hours in the afternoon. This was when we could swim or canoe or do anything else in any area that was not being used by the Scouts in camp.

By the time I had finished supper duty about seven-thirty, I would have worked from nine to eleven hours in a day. I easily figured out why I wasn't being paid for that job. The entire Boy Scouts of America didn't have that kind of money!

Maybe it wouldn't have happened if I had had a different tentmate. Or maybe it would have happened but would have started later. Whatever might have been true in other circumstances did not keep me from starting to get sick near the end of the second of the ten weeks.

It was not like a cold or the flu. There was no headache, though there was some upset stomach that went with it. It was a strange sickness, unlike anything that I had ever experienced or thought about experiencing before: I was starting to get homesick!

At first I started missing my brother, Joe. At night, when I would be lying in bed trying not to think about snakes, I would remember all of the times he and I lay just across the room from one another, talking about things of the day just past and our plans for tomorrow. My memories were perhaps sweeter than the realities. But I soon terribly missed my brother.

The following week it got even worse. I started missing Daddy. I could hear the sound of his voice as he told us stories about his childhood. It got so bad that I even had fond memories of times that he had punished me! Even my father's punishments seemed more desirable than sharing a tent with Bobby Jensen and working in the kitchen all day.

That Thursday, the sickness took a turn for the worse.

Thursday was all-day-hike day. It was the best day of the week for being kitchen steward. Early in the morning we packed sack lunches of boiled eggs and peanut butter and jelly sandwiches, then all of the Boy Scouts in camp headed out for the day. There was no lunch duty, and I could join any group for an all-day-hike either to Shining Rock or over Cold Mountain.

On that day I had joined a scout troop from Canton, and the Scoutmaster was a man named Mr. Cooper. As we walked along, he wanted to know who I was. I told him, and that set him off for the day.

He had been a young Boy Scout in my daddy's troop when Daddy was the Scoutmaster. All of the rest of the day he talked about my daddy: what a wonderful man he was, all the things he had taught the boys, the stories he had told them, the times he had stood up for them. The more he talked, the more homesick I got. I had to pretend that I was allergic to ragweed, blowing my nose a lot to cover up the fact that I was crying all the way back to camp.

The following week the illness became almost fatally acute. I actually started missing my mama. And for a thirteen-year-old boy, that is about as low as you can go!

Mrs. Deerbone, the cook for whom I worked in the kitchen, had gone to elementary school with Mama at Fines Creek. Now she couldn't stop talking about Mama and all the wonderful things they had done together when they were growing up. I thought that I was going to die!

As I think back on it, I am sure that some good and wonderful things did happen at camp that summer. I did learn to swim, and I got to canoe so much that later on I built a canoe of my own. I did get to shoot—not only bows and arrows, but even rifles at the rifle range. I did hike a lot, and I even learned a lot about cooking (and I am one of the world's best pot washers). And Bobby Jensen got fired after four weeks, so I got both a decent tentmate and a better kitchen helper with whom to work. But I spent most of the summer in the dire straits of homesickness that had me counting—not only the weeks then days, but finally the hours then minutes until it would all be over and I could get back to my family again.

Finally the day came. It was a Sunday afternoon, one workday after the last group of scouts had left the morning before.

My stuff was all packed, and I was standing beside the road in front of the main lodge when I spotted the green Plymouth coming up the gravel road. Mama and Daddy were in the front, and I could see Joe leaning over the back of the front seat and up between their shoulders.

I ran to the car, threw my stuff on the back seat, and jumped in. "Let's go!" I said.

"Have you checked out?" Mama asked. "Have you said goodbye to everyone?"

"Did that last week! Let's go!" And we headed for home.

The picnic basket was beside me on the back seat. It was filled with food Mama had fixed. It had in it Mama's fried chicken, Mama's deviled eggs, Mama's lemonade, Mama's lemon pie. Halfway home, we stopped beside the road and had a great picnic! Then we went on home.

When Daddy pulled into the driveway, I started to jump out of the car, but Mama stopped me. "Wait a minute," she said. "We have a surprise for you."

"What is it?" I honestly asked. I was home. I didn't need anything else!

"You know that bedroom we always call the guest room?" she asked. "Well, this summer we got rid of that old furniture in there. We also painted it a nice blue color, and it is now your room! We've even moved your bed in there and put half of the books and toys in there too! Isn't that a great surprise? You have a room of your own!"

When I looked at Joe, he wasn't smiling. In fact, the look on his face told me that I was not the only one who had missed his brother this summer. I thought carefully, and then said, "Mama, I already have a room of my own. It's been my room since before my brother was born! It's a good room, and I'm used to it! I think I better stay in my own room instead of messing up another one. Besides, I need to be there to take care of my brother in case he needs me in the night!"

No one argued. They just watched as Joe and I worked together all afternoon moving all of my things back into our room, where they had always belonged, so that, just about dark, we were ready to go to sleep in our room.

Am I my brother's keeper? You bet I am!

FRIENDS COME BACK

Davey Martin was not one of my first childhood friends. In fact, we did not even meet until we were in junior high school. We had each gone to different elementary schools on opposite sides of town. Still, the preparation for our friendship had begun when Davey was two weeks old.

It happened like this: when Davey was thirteen days old, his mother was carrying him in her arms nursing him when she had a massive cerebral hemorrhage, fell dead to the floor, and Davey rolled out of her arms. This was the reason that Davey Martin was raised by his grandmother, whom he called Mazza, a laughing woman who had already raised a whole family of her own, including Davey's mother, who was now dead.

Having raised her own children, Mazza knew that, in any garden, the weeds are always as healthy as the corn. So Davey was free to grow like a weed!

The first time I went home with him, when we were in the seventh grade, Davey and I were planning a hike together on a mountain above town. We told Mazza our plan, and she just listened. As we left, Mazza asked us no questions about time or our plans. She just said, "I guess you boys know what you're doing. I'll see you when you get home!"

I couldn't believe it! I had never in my life heard anything like this! No problems, no objections, no questions! We were on our own!

Davey and I became friends because each of us had something that the other one needed. Sometimes Davey needed a mama who strongly disapproved of everything he did. I had one of those. Sometimes I needed a grandmother who did not care what I did. He had one of those! We put the two of them together, drifted back and forth from my house to his house as needed, and all was well. He and I spent almost every spare moment with one another.

Davey and I were such close friends that, in high school, we never double-dated. No, we took turns dating, and the one who had no date was the driver for the one who did!

We made my mama's green Plymouth into a limousine by pinning one edge of a long beach towel across the headliner just above the back edge of the front seat and pinning the bottom edge of the same towel to the seat back. Now, driver in the front, daters in the privacy of the back, we were on the way! There were actually times when we picked girls up for dates, and when they saw the car, they turned and ran back inside their own houses and refused to come out!

One day Mazza and my mother were visiting and talking about—of course—Davey and me. They went on and on about what good friends we were and how close we were to one another.

Finally, as a way of summing up the conversation, Mama said to Mazza: "Those boys are so much alike, why, I guess they're just like two peas in a pod!" Since both of them had grown up as farm girls, it was an apt metaphor.

Mazza laughed out loud, then came back with her own comparison. "You can think that if you want to, but if you ask me, I'd say they were more like two cowpiles in a barnyard!"

My mother, a woman who did not appreciate even the odor of impropriety, winced and blushed. "That's terrible!" She said to Mazza. "How can you say a thing like that about our boys?"

Mazza laughed again. "Because it's true!" she answered. "Those boys are so close that neither one of them knows when the other one stinks! And if you have a friend like that when you're thirteen years old, that's a *fine* thing!"

Our favorite thing to do together all through our years of friendship was to go camping and hiking. We started going camping together, all by ourselves, when we were thirteen years old in the seventh grade, and we continued all the way through high school. After all, sleeping in the woods was more attractive than sleeping at home.

One of Davey's relatives had an old log cabin high up on the mountain above Sulpher Springs. Our families would let the two of us hike up the mountain, carrying our own food and sleeping bags, and camp out there. Sometime we took other friends, but friends or not, Davey and I went camping every possible chance we got.

"How do we know that it's safe for the boys to go up there?" Mama one day asked Daddy when Davey and I were announcing our plans. He and I were packing our food for our third Friday night trip in three weeks, and Mama was convinced that this much fun must surely be overdoing something!

"It's safe enough for you," Daddy answered her. "There aren't any girls up there."

On one of our trips, Mama had driven us to the base of the mountain and let us out to start our hike to the cabin. One of Davey's uncles was passing by on his tractor, and he stopped to talk with us. "Why are you boys carrying those heavy sleeping bags all the way up there? Those beds up in the cabin are all made up with sheets and quilts on them. You don't need those sleeping bags!"

Davey replied, "We've seen those sheets and quilts! I think

that the same ones have been on those beds since nineteen-and-twenty-nine! We sleep in our own sleeping bags on top of the covers!"

The old cabin was one room with two old beds at one end and a fireplace at the other end. Since the whole cabin was homemade, the fireplace didn't draw well. We would gather wood and build a big fire to keep us warm for the night. Then we would sit by the fire and, just as we began to get warm, we would start choking from the smoke and have to open the door so the fireplace would draw. After that we would stand by the door and take deep breaths until we were freezing to death. Then the cycle would repeat itself over and over again until we gave up and went to bed.

Looking back, it is hard to even imagine what Davey and I must have smelled like when we returned home after several days of cabin camping. We usually hiked down the mountain and ended up at my house first, since it was the closest. Mama would be looking out the window, waiting to stop us before we could bring our accumulated odors into her clean house.

She would meet us in the yard and stop us. "You boys don't come in the house. Come on in the garage now. I will close the garage door and not look while both of you boys take off all of those stinky clothes and run for the shower."

Davey and I would take off our clothes in the garage and

truly run for the shower. As we left Mama in the garage with the dirty clothes, Davey would chant, "We don't stink, we're cowpiles. We don't stink, we're cowpiles," and Mama would growl at him. We would all three laugh, and Davey and I would see Mama's little grin even through the frown she tried to put on for us.

By the time we were in the ninth grade, our camping adventures were ranging farther and turning into actual backpacking. I had, by now, spent a summer working at Boy Scout camp, and we had turned fourteen years old. At about this time, one of our neighbors, Mr. Jay Howard, opened the whole world of the Great Smoky Mountains National Park to us.

Mr. Howard was the neighborhood mailman, and since he and his wife had no children, he was like an extra father to all of us. One day, Davey and I were loading up our packs to go to the cabin when Mr. Howard came by delivering the mail.

"You boys like the woods, don't you?" he said. "I love the woods myself. Why don't the three of us do some serious hiking in the Smokies?"

Starting that very weekend, Davey and I went in Mr. Howard's truck into the Smokies, and we began exploring trails and mountains. Gradually, we covered all of the Appalachian Trail from north to south in the park and even beyond, and over time, we hiked and camped on miles of side trails off the main trail itself.

One weekend Mr. Howard told us that he was finally ready to take us to his favorite place. School was out for the summer, so we could go any time Mr. Howard was off from the post office. It was Friday morning when we loaded our packs in the pickup truck.

As we left my house, Mama said, "I hope you know what you're doing."

As we left Davey's house, Mazza said, "I'll see you when you get home!"

Mr. Howard didn't tell us where we were going. He drove us through Maggie Valley and across Soco Gap over into Cherokee. We went through Cherokee and headed into the Great Smoky Mountains National Park toward Gatlinburg.

The pickup climbed the mountain to Newfound Gap, where we parked on the North Carolina–Tennessee state line. "Let's go!" Mr. Howard said. We loaded our packs on our backs and started north on the Appalachian Trail.

We had hiked this part of the trail many times. We loved to camp at Ice Water Springs and hike to the magnificent overlook called Charlie's Bunion. This was familiar, at least at first. Three miles up the Appalachian Trail, though, we turned left on a trail we had never traveled before. The sign read, BOULEVARD TRAIL. After dropping in elevation for the first half-mile or so, the trail leveled and beautifully followed a long ridge, up and down, up and down.

After about four miles, we started a long climb that seemed to never end. We passed through fragrant fir trees and finally came out on top of Mt. LeConte—at 6,593 feet, one of the highest peaks in the Smokies. The mountain turned out to be even more remarkable in that, instead of being part of a chain, it stands out all by itself with a 360-degree view, perfect from every lookout and in every direction.

We stayed two days on Mt. LeConte, camping at the three-sided trail shelter built of native rock and located about half a mile below the summit of the mountain. Each evening, we hiked out to the western ledge of Cliff Tops, where we watched the orange and purple colors of the setting sun as it burned its way down behind the mountains of Tennessee. Each morning, before daylight, we hiked to the eastern rocks of Myrtle Point, where we watched the newborn blues and yellows of the rising sun as it melted its way up out of the valleys of North Carolina.

It was a place of pure magic to two outdoors-loving fourteen-year-old boys.

During each day we saw deer as tame as cows and visited

the 1927 lodge, a cluster of log cabins a half-mile below the trail shelter, where, from spring until fall, those who were lucky enough to get a reservation and willing enough to pay the price could spend the night in bunk beds and eat food packed in each week by mule without having to carry either sleeping gear or food on the hike to the mountaintop.

On the second morning, after we had cooked our breakfast over the fire, Mr. Howard took us down from the mountain on the Alum Cave Bluff trail, a steep trail with fascinating geology and spectacular views.

After that trip, Davey and I joined the long list of others who had come to consider LeConte their own "private mountain." We went there every chance we got, and we stayed as long as we could each time we went.

Not yet old enough to drive ourselves, we were at first dependent upon parents and relatives to take us to a trail head, then come back to get us on the right day at the right time. Before long, however, we discovered a way we could be on our own.

Interstate 40 had not yet been built through the mountains from North Carolina to Tennessee, and the only way to get through the Smokies was to take old US 441, which then ran directly through the park from Cherokee to Gatlinburg. Davey and I discovered that we could buy a bus ticket from Sulpher

Springs to Gatlinburg and get on the bus with our loaded backpacks. Then we would pull the bell cord to get off as the bus passed where one of the trail heads left the highway.

We would pull the cord at Newfound Gap and the driver would say, "You can't get off here. This is the middle of nowhere!"

"That's just the point!" we would answer as we jumped off the bus with our backpacks.

We had learned the bus schedule so that when we came back down, we could intercept another bus, flag it down, and buy a cash ticket to ride back home. The bus drivers didn't seem to care that we smelled like cowpiles as long as we had enough money to buy a ticket to Sulpher Springs.

By the time Davey and I were sixteen, we could drive, and as often as we could borrow a car that could stay out for a couple of days or more before being returned, we headed for Mt. LeConte.

By the time we were out of high school, we had made more than forty trips to the mountain using, at various times, each of the five different trails that led to the top. Our trips knew no seasons; we went all through the year, once measuring a snow depth of thirty inches outside the shelter as we stoked the fire inside, feeling warmer though there was no wall on the fourth side.

As time passed, more and more people began to hike and camp all over the Smokies, and we gradually had to learn to share our space. Even the old lodge added more cabins, and as many as fifty people each night could sleep and be fed there in the open season of the year. With more people, the visible bear population increased. The bears were drawn to the aromas and tastes of available human food. In response, the Park Service closed the open wall of the trail shelter with a chain-link fence and a chain-link door that could be shut and latched.

On one trip, Davey and I came over the top of the mountain on the Boulevard Trail. As we headed down toward the shelter, we heard the voices of girls screaming. Once the shelter was in sight, we saw what the problem was. There was a troop of Girl Scouts inside the shelter with the chain-link gate closed and latched. On the outside stood a large black bear, hind feet on the ground, standing upright with his front paws on the fence, enjoying looking at the Girl Scouts who were trapped in the people zoo!

Davey and I made one last trip to our mountain at the end of the summer after we graduated from high school. When the two of us went our separate ways to college, we were already talking about and looking forward to return camping trips the next summer.

I did not go home for Thanksgiving my freshman year in

college. I was on a class field trip to Washington, D.C. So Christmas ended up being my first visit home for any time longer than a quick weekend. Davey was, of course, also home.

In the span of one college semester, the two of us had both become so smart that we could hardly stand to be around our families. We did pretty well with the party schedule leading up to Christmas itself, but once Christmas day itself had passed, we faced a long week with nothing interesting at all to do until the new year arrived and we could return to school.

To this day I honestly do not know who first had the idea, but suddenly, we had a plan: "Let's go to LeConte camping. That'll be great!"

Though we had been to the mountain in all seasons of the year, winter was no easy time to be there. Snow and lots of ice on the trails and excessively cold wind were more normal than unusual at this time of the year. The days were short and the nights were long.

Later that day, when Mr. Howard came by our house delivering the mail, we told him about our plan. "I'll tell you what, boys," he started. "This is what you should do. You know the old lodge up there is closed in the wintertime. But Herrick Brown, who runs the lodge, is a good friend of mine. I know that you could probably go by his house in Gatlinburg and get a key to one of the buildings up there, and then you could sleep inside in the lodge. That way you wouldn't have to carry so much stuff, and you won't freeze to death in the trail shelter."

It was a great idea, so Davey and I started in with our plans to leave two days later.

Mazza said exactly what we knew she would say: "I know you boys know what you're doing. I'll see you when you get home."

Mama also said exactly what we knew she would say: "You boys are going to die! You are going to freeze to death and we will have wasted all of the money we paid to send you to college this year. And since we've already paid for the spring semester, that money will really be wasted, and they won't give it back! You'll freeze to death, and they won't find your bodies until the springtime, and when they do, I won't cry. No, I'll just say, 'I told them. I told them!'"

After that, Davey and I had to go, whether we wanted to or not.

On Thursday morning, the day after Christmas, we got up early—nine o'clock (we were, after all, college freshmen)—loaded our camping stuff in the trunk of Mama's car, and headed off into the Smokies.

It was nearly eleven o'clock when we got to Herrick Brown's house outside of Gatlinburg, where we planned to get a key to some part of the lodge. But when we got to the Browns' house, they were not at home. Being college freshmen, it had not occurred to us that we needed to take some responsibility in making the key-borrowing plan. We just assumed that the Browns sat around at home all day every day, simply waiting in case some college boys might come by wanting to borrow a key to the lodge.

"They must have gone to the store," Davey said. "Let's go down into town and get something to eat, and by then they'll probably be home." We did, but when we returned about noontime, the Browns were nowhere to be seen.

Pretty soon we were forced to make a decision: should we head on up the mountain and camp in the trail shelter as we had done so many times before (and possibly freeze to death), or should we give up, go back home, and tell my mama she was right?

It was not a difficult decision!

It was a little bit past noon when Davey and I parked Mama's Plymouth in the Cherokee Orchard parking lot above Gatlinburg, loaded up our backpacks and all of the camping gear we had brought, and headed up the Rainbow Falls trail. On one of the shortest days of the year, we were starting up a trail that climbed 3,800 feet in about seven miles, and just as we started up the trail, snow started to fall from a heavily overcast sky.

Less than an hour up the trail, we had gained enough altitude so that we were now walking on old snow, snow from the last week's snowfall, snow that had partially melted and then refrozen so that it made a perfectly slick base for the new snow that was now falling more rapidly with each minute that passed.

By the end of the second hour, we had come to Rainbow Falls, the waterfall from which the trail took its name. Only, on this day, instead of a waterfall, there was a solid frozen column of ice from cliff top to creek bed. The frozen waterfall had a clear blue streak on one side of the ice column, and Davey and I wondered aloud whether this beautiful but strange thing we were seeing might be somehow related to the origin of the name, Rainbow Falls.

After a snack break at the base of the frozen waterfall, the two of us, both students at fine colleges that trained the mind in higher critical thinking skills, made a brilliant decision: "Let's keep going!"

So we headed up the last four miles of the trail, sliding back two steps for every three or four we took, with no more than two hours of daylight left in the heavily overcast, snowy day.

As the trail moved up the mountainside, it turned back and forth, back and forth, in long switchbacks across the steep slope in order to gain altitude more gently and efficiently. As we followed the trail on its back-and-forth route, Davey and I noticed something.

Some time earlier, Herrick Brown, who ran the lodge, had come up with two old crank generator telephones. He had one set up at the lodge on top of the mountain and the other down at his house in Gatlinburg, not too long a distance as the crow flies for them to work. The two telephones where connected by a single wire that ran straight down the mountainside from tree trunk to tree trunk. As Davey and I walked back and forth on the switchback trail, we would, from time to time, pass under the telephone line. The third time this happened, we made our second brilliant decision of the day: "Why are we walking back and forth on this long, drawn-out trail when that telephone line goes straight up to the lodge? If we would forget the old trail and follow the wire, we would surely be there in no time!"

So in the last half-hour of daylight, we plunged off the trail, looking up to follow the wire as we plodded into snow that was just thick enough on the ground to cover the big holes and drops between rocks and logs into which our legs fell once we put the weight of a step on the snow.

As darkness crept up on us, we found ourselves floundering, now far enough from the trail that it seemed no harder to go on than to try to find our way back to where we had left our safe and clear route.

On the very edge of darkness, we made our third brilliant decision: "Let's split up!" As I look back on that day, I wonder how two eighteen-year-olds with these kinds of critical thinking skills ever got accepted into any college at all.

Our strategy was for me to stay put, try to build a fire, and establish a "base camp." (We had heard that term, but we had no idea what we were talking about!) Davey would, against the last fading light of the sky, attempt to follow the wire to see if we were perhaps getting close to the lodge after all.

I watched Davey disappear into the dark trees, and as I listened to the sound of his steps in the snow fading into silence, I could, from over fifty miles away, begin to hear the sound of my mother's voice: *"You're going to die. You're going to die."*

I tried to build a fire, but every stick of wood that came out of the snow was so water-soaked that it folded instead of breaking. I used every match I had brought in an attempt to ignite a small piece of birch bark that never did decide it would like to burn.

Finally I gave up and knew that we were in real trouble. My buddy was gone, my mama was right, and when they found our frozen bodies in the springtime, everyone would know how dumb we were because we wouldn't even be dead in the same place trying to help one another.

First I whimpered, then I shivered with cold, and finally I gave over to surrendered sobbing. Suddenly, through my own crying, I heard another sound: someone was calling my name. When I looked up toward the sound, there, through the dark trees, I saw a light. It was Davey coming back.

As it turned out, we were actually less than a mile from the lodge. Davey had made it there and broken into the dining hall, where he had found an old Coleman lantern and a pair of decorative snowshoes on the wall. With the lantern in his hand and the snowshoes on his feet, he had come back to get me.

My crying was out of control now. "I thought I'd never see you again. I thought you weren't coming back. I thought we were both going to die. I thought I had lost my guide. I thought—"

Davey had had enough, "Shut up!" he said, "I'm not your guide. I'm nothing but your friend, and friends come back—they don't have any choice."

The two of us gathered up all of my part of the stuff and retraced Davey's snowshoe tracks back up to the lodge. We ate and slept in the kitchen of the old dining hall, safe at last from my mother's dire predictions of death.

I have no recollection of the hike down the mountain the next day nor of the drive over the mountains back home. But I do remember that, when we drove up to my house, the first thing that we saw was Mama's face in the window, exactly where we had last seen her watch us as we had left the morning before.

Davey and I were ready for her when we walked into the house. "Oh, I am so glad to see you! I know you had a terrible time! I know you didn't sleep a bit, did you? I just know you both nearly froze to death!"

Davey grinned. I just deadpanned Mama and answered flatly: "We knew what we were doing. We had a great time, didn't wake up all night. We might go back tomorrow. We've done this before. Besides, we're eighteen years old and we are in college!"

That was the last time Davey Martin and I went to Mt. LeConte for thirty-five years.

In October of 1998, my wife and I were in New Zealand, so we didn't know until we got back from the trip about what had happened. It was on a Sunday afternoon that Davey's wife had taken him to the hospital because he was "not feeling well." As they walked into the emergency room, Davey suffered cardiac arrest. He awakened seven hours later after angioplasty and a jumpstart.

For the next two years Davey did everything right—eating, medication, rest, exercise. The question he asked at checkups in the doctor's office was always the same: "When can I go hiking again?"

The answer changed as Davey progressed. First it was, "Don't be out of reach of the telephone," then gradually longer and longer (measured in miles now) walks were allowed.

At the end of two years, I got a call from Davey. "I'm going to the doctor next week, and if everything is really all right, he says that I will be free to hike anywhere as far as I want to go!"

I didn't tell him, but I got on the telephone and called LeConte Lodge and made four reservations (we were couples now) for two nights on the first days that were open.

A week later, Davey called again. "I passed!" he reported, "The doctor says I'm free to go anywhere!"

"Guess where we're going?" I asked him. Then I told him about the plans I had made for the four of us to go to LeConte. "It didn't kill us the last time," I said, "so let's go try it again!"

We were to travel separately, again to Gatlinburg, where we would meet to hike up the mountain. On the drive over, I passed through my hometown and stopped to see my mother. She was in a nursing home now, in what would turn out to be the last months of her life. Sometimes her thoughts were jumbled, but most of the time she was as clear as could be. I hoped that this would be one of the clear days.

I parked the car outside the home, went inside, and walked down the hall to Mama's room. She was stretched, half-propped, on her bed. There, in a chair beside the bed, also visiting, was her long-time friend, Mrs. Cole. We visited briefly, catching up on the news, and then I decided to tell Mama where I was going.

"Guess what, Mama?" I teased her. "I'm on the way to Gatlinburg. David and I are going to Mt. LeConte. I'm on the way to meet him right now!"

I looked at Mama. It was obvious that she was thinking, but she was not saying anything.

It was Mrs. Cole who spoke to her. "Lucille," she started, "are you going to let those two boys do that?"

Mama smiled, "They know what they're doing," she answered. "They've done it before."

Mrs. Cole picked back up, "I was so worried when David had that heart attack. I was scared to death that he was going to die!"

"Oh, no," Mama said, "he wouldn't die. Donald wasn't there. I don't think that one of them could die without the other one's being there."

"They always were close," Mrs. Cole finished her thoughts. "Close as brothers. I guess that they were just about like two peas in a pod."

Mama propped herself higher up on her elbows. "Un-uuh!" she shook her head. "I'd say they were more like two cowpiles beside a barn!"

Mrs. Cole flushed. "Lucille, I can't believe that you said that!"

"Well, it's true," Mama settled back down. "They're so much alike that neither one of them knows when the other one stinks! And when you have a friend like that for more than forty years, that's a fine thing!"

LOSING MY NAME

Being born is one time about which I have no memory at all! As far as I am concerned, I was not there. The whole thing was missed by me until it was all over. What I do know and remember are my mother's stories of my birth. I heard the stories of a horrible forceps delivery, told over and over again.

The nature of this experience gave me the name by which my mother called me all through the first days, weeks, months, and even years of my life: "My Baby!"

Two-and-a-half years later, my brother, Joe, was born in Asheville by an on-time Caesarian. He got a name: "Joe." I remained "My Baby!"

I still remember the first day of school in Mrs. Ledbetter's room at Sulpher Springs School. Mrs. Ledbetter was calling the roll of students, and I listened to the names and the students' answers: "Charlotte Abernathy." "Here." "Harold Allen." "Here." "Ray Ammons." "Here." On down the list she went until she came to "Donald Davis."

Somewhere I had heard this name, but it had not been used enough for me to respond to it immediately. When I sat there and said nothing, Mrs. Ledbetter prompted me: "You are supposed to say either 'here' or 'present.'"

"Present!" I said loudly, for I thought that a present was exactly what I had just been given. I had my own name, "Donald Douglas Davis," and I loved it! I said "present" every single day when the roll was called all through the first grade.

The name lasted for exactly one year. The next year, the year that I was to enter the second grade, my mama went back to teaching, and she came to teach at Sulpher Springs School. My name was now gone. Instead of "Donald Davis," I now became "Mrs. Davis's little boy." I hated the new name. Everywhere I heard it, from students and teachers alike: "That's Mrs. Davis's little boy. He's not in his mama's room, he's in Miss Lois Harrold's room—Mrs. Davis's little boy."

That same year that Mama started back teaching, Mr. Lawrence Leatherwood was the principal of Sulpher Springs School. Sulpher Springs School was a big, consolidated, rural-county school with four classes in each grade level from first through sixth grades. Yet in addition to being principal, Mr. Leatherwood was also a full-time sixth-grade teacher.

Mr. Leatherwood's son, Larry, was also a student at Sulpher Springs School. He was one year younger than I was, so it was not until the following year that Larry Leatherwood ended up in my mama's room in the second grade.

Larry was a big, active boy. He would be a handful for anyone. His being the principal's son made Mama even more nervous about having Larry as her student. She was always afraid she might do something wrong.

One day we were all eating lunch in the school lunchroom. I was at the table with Miss Metcalf's class. Mama was at the table beside us with her class. Suddenly we heard a clattering sound—*whock*—from Mama's table. Everyone who heard it looked and saw that Larry had knocked over his glass milk bottle and spilled chocolate milk all over the table.

While everyone watched, Mama quickly got up from her chair and headed for the kitchen to get a rag from Mrs. Calhoun so she could wipe up the mess. As she emerged from the kitchen door, she saw Larry standing beside the table. He had pulled his shirttail out of his pants, had used it to wipe up the milk, and was now stuffing the entire wet mess back down into his britches.

That night, at supper, Mama started talking to Daddy. "Let me tell you what happened at school today," she smiled. I knew that her story was going to be about the cafeteria adventures of Larry Leatherwood. Mama's story started, "Mr. Leatherwood's *little boy* . . ." I think that in my own mind that was the day that Larry Leatherwood and I became good friends!

I was "Mrs. Davis's little boy," and he was "Mr. Leatherwood's little boy." We both hated it!

One day, later on in that year, there was a teachers' meeting after school. Mama and Mr. Leatherwood decided to park Larry and me in Mama's room for the duration of the meeting. They put the two of us in the room with only two words of oral instruction: "Be have!"

As soon as the two of them were gone, Larry and I started experimenting with the room to see what we could do that was interesting and would make the time pass more quickly. The desks in the room were screwed to the floor. Larry showed me how you could get up on top of the desks and actually step from one to the other. You could even run around all over the room jumping from desktop to desktop!

He and I were running up and down the rows of desks chasing one another, jumping back and forth from row to row and having a great time! There were only two things that we did not notice. We did not notice that every time we took a big jump, our rubber heels made black marks on the desktops! We also did not notice that the teachers' meeting was over!

The door opened, and we were caught by both parents at the same time.

This was followed by a long and excruciating ordeal while Larry and I had to sit and listen to a debate about "who should spank whom." In the end, a decision was made. It was decided that my mama should spank Larry, since she was his teacher, and that Mr. Leatherwood should spank me, since he was my principal. After all, this was an issue of trouble at school, not trouble at home.

They made the two of us stand side by side and bend over two of the very desktops on which we had been running. Then they counted together: "One"—*pop*—"two"—*pop*—all the way up to five. It was from insult as much as from pain that we suffered.

Later on that afternoon, when we got home, Larry and I both learned, separately, why the decision had been made in that way. After what had happened at school, we could now get another spanking at home. This time, Larry got spanked by his daddy, and I got spanked by my mama. The two of us also discovered that the count at home had gone all the way up to ten!

Larry and I knew that when we got to junior high school, we would fade into anonymity and get our names back. We looked forward to the seventh grade with passion. But the year I got to the seventh grade, Mr. Leatherwood became the superintendent of the entire school system—and it seemed that everyone there also knew my mama! We never did get our names back.

The summer of the year that I moved from the sixth grade to the seventh grade, we moved to our new house. As it turned out, the new house was backyard-to-backyard adjacent to the Leatherwoods' house.

Now it was Mama who got promoted! No, she still taught second grade at Sulpher Springs School. Her promotion was that she was an extra mother, for life, to Larry! Neither he nor I ever escaped any of our parents! Now both of us had two sets, and we never could get away with much of anything.

My mama and Larry's mama raised us by talking and crying over the fence between the two backyards. It took hours and hours of talk for two mamas to raise, mold, correct, mourn, and adjust a total of four boys. Larry and I did not realize at the time that my brother, Joe, and his brother, Ronnie, were as much a topic of discussion as we were.

Larry and I went off our separate ways to college, while Mama kept teaching at Sulpher Springs School. After college, Larry became a teacher in the same system we had both attended as children, I left the town of my childhood, and Mama kept teaching.

At the end of the summer of 1981, I got a telephone call from Mama. It was, she reported, the opening day of the school year in the forty-second year of her teaching career. "Guess what?" she said.

"I don't know what," I answered. "Tell me."

"I'm going to retire!" She surprised me totally.

"You mean you're not teaching this year? When did you decide that?" I couldn't believe it.

"No," she went on, "I'm teaching this year. Today was the first day of school. I have a great group of kids. But I have decided that this is going to be my last year."

"How did you decide that? You've sure been there long enough. It's time for you to stop."

"Well," I could almost hear the smile in her voice, "this summer we got a new school superintendent. I think that he thinks he's a Methodist Bishop or something. He decided to move all of the principals around—without talking to any-body or asking anybody anything about it as far as any of us can tell." I kept listening.

"We got to school today and found out that we have a new principal at Sulpher Springs School. You'll never guess who it is, so I'll just tell you. It's *Larry Leatherwood!*"

"That's great, Mama!" I was excited for her.

"That's what you think," I was listening again to the laughter in her voice. "We had our first teachers' meeting this afternoon, and every time Larry told us to do something, all I could do was close my eyes and see a little seven-year-old-boy standing beside the table wiping up chocolate milk with his shirttail! I told him when the meeting was over that, after this year, it will be time for me to stay home!"

It was a good decision! In the years of my mother's retirement, Larry went on to become one of the associate superintendents in that same system his father had headed.

———

In the spring of 1998, my mother died. She was sick for less than the last year of her eighty-year life.

After her death, my brother and I were planning her funeral and the topic of pallbearers came up. There were half-enough grandsons to fill out the needed number, and we were trying to figure out what neighbors or other relatives were appropriate (and young enough to walk).

All of a sudden, my wife, Merle, said, "What about Mr. Leatherwood's little boy?" We all laughed, but we also knew that Larry was the perfect one to ask.

I called, and Larry agreed. So Larry Leatherwood, my mama's student, her extra son, her neighbor, her fellow teacher, her last principal, her lifelong friend, helped bear her last remains to their peaceful resting place.

We were finishing up at the cemetery when, someone out of sight spoke to me. "Dr. Davis?" they said. In the same moment, when I did not quite recognize that they were actually calling for me, I heard another voice directed at Larry say, "Dr. Leatherwood?"

All of a sudden, I thought, *We got so smart we lost our names again, didn't we, Larry?*

When we were finished at the cemetery, Larry and I met back at our two boyhood houses, talking all through the afternoon over the fence between the backyards. We spent most of our conversation traveling on the free ticket of remembering: the time we got two spankings, the time our daddies got real fireworks for the fourth of July, sledding down the pasture hill in many winters . . . We traveled for years in one afternoon!

When it was time to each go his own way, one of us said, "Don't you wish we could go back? Don't you wish we could go back to those days when we hated what everybody called us, but we didn't have to pay any of the bills? Don't you wish we could go back, for just one week?"

Then suddenly both of us realized that we had, through the unlimited magic of memory and storytelling, just been back! We had traveled through dozens of lives and scores of years in one short afternoon. We also realized that, through that same magic, we could keep on traveling as far and as free, watching from any side we chose, anytime and every time we stopped to remember and to tell our stories.